M.M 2013-oct   M.M

AUG - - 2013

SPECIAL MESSAGE TO READERS

THE ULVERSCROFT FOUNDATION
(registered UK charity number 264873)
was established in 1972 to provide funds for research, diagnosis and treatment of eye diseases. Examples of major projects funded by the Ulverscroft Foundation are:-

- The Children's Eye Unit at Moorfields Eye Hospital, London
- The Ulverscroft Children's Eye Unit at Great Ormond Street Hospital for Sick Children
- Funding research into eye diseases and treatment at the Department of Ophthalmology, University of Leicester
- The Ulverscroft Vision Research Group, Institute of Child Health
- Twin operating theatres at the Western Ophthalmic Hospital, London
- The Chair of Ophthalmology at the Royal Australian College of Ophthalmologists

You can help further the work of the Foundation by making a donation or leaving a legacy. Every contribution is gratefully received. If you would like to help support the Foundation or require further information, please contact:

**THE ULVERSCROFT FOUNDATION
The Green, Bradgate Road, Anstey
Leicester LE7 7FU, England
Tel: (0116) 236 4325**

website: www.foundation.ulverscroft.com

A TIME FOR DREAMS

Claire is a teacher awaiting an Ofsted inspection at her school. She discovers that the chief inspector is her former fiancé, Adam, whom she has not seen for five years. Although Claire is now in a relationship with Martin, she is overcome with guilt when she realises she still has feelings for Adam. Suddenly she has to confront her past and decisions have to be made.

Books by Dawn Bridge
in the Linford Romance Library:

JOURNEY TO PARADISE

DAWN BRIDGE

A TIME
FOR DREAMS

Complete and Unabridged

LINFORD
Leicester

ST. THOMAS PUBLIC LIBRARY

First published in Great Britain in 2011

First Linford Edition
published 2013

Copyright © 2011 by Dawn Bridge
All rights reserved

A catalogue record for this book is available
from the British Library.

ISBN 978–1–4448–1610–5

Published by
F. A. Thorpe (Publishing)
Anstey, Leicestershire

Set by Words & Graphics Ltd.
Anstey, Leicestershire
Printed and bound in Great Britain by
T. J. International Ltd., Padstow, Cornwall

This book is printed on acid-free paper

Too Many Memories

'Claire, I've missed you so much.' Martin James flung open the door to his penthouse flat, threw his arms around the petite young woman, lifting her off the ground in his enthusiasm to kiss her.

'Put me down,' she gasped. You nearly crushed me. Let's go inside, Martin. All your neighbours will be watching.'

'I don't care. What's wrong with a chap kissing his girlfriend, especially when he hasn't seen her for days?'

'Nothing, but we don't want an audience.'

'OK. How was your first week in the new job?'

'Stressful, but the children were nice.'

With his arm still around her, Martin led Claire into the lounge and sat her down saying, 'You must be tired after all that driving. I'll make some coffee. Then I'll start on the lunch. Are you hungry?'

'Not really. Can I help you?'

'No, you relax. I can manage.' He strode into the kitchen.

Claire gazed out of the window at the breathtaking view over London. Then she sank back against the luxurious cushioned sofa, glad to do as Martin suggested. She was tired, but not from driving. She'd had a sleepless night.

Claire glanced around the opulent room, so different from the lounge in her tiny flat. Martin has very good taste she thought. Claire closed her eyes, mulling over the events of the past few weeks before drifting off to sleep.

She had known Martin for five months. He'd been a fellow guest at a friend's engagement party. She couldn't help noticing him. He was taller than everyone else, extremely smart and good looking. All the unattached women seemed drawn to him, but it was Claire he was interested in. They got on well together from the start and when he'd asked her to go out with him, she'd agreed.

Martin was the manager of one of the leading banks in London. At thirty-four he was five years older than Claire. They enjoyed the same leisure activities, eating out, visiting art galleries, museums and going to the cinema and concerts. All things Claire had only been able to do infrequently as her teacher's salary didn't stretch that far. Living in London was very expensive.

However, just before meeting Martin, Claire had applied for another teaching post in the small country town of Greenhill about an hour's drive from London. When she'd seen the vacancy she'd seized the opportunity and sent in her application immediately, thinking it would give her the chance to get away from London.

Claire had dreamed of living in Greenhill for so long. She'd been successful and was offered the job which would start at the beginning of the next school year in September. When Martin found out he was opposed to Claire moving away from London, but she insisted that there was nothing she could do about it. It was settled and she would have to go.

'But I'll miss you,' Martin had protested.

'I'll miss you too, but I've had enough of working in London. I'll still be able to see you at weekends. I'm not going to the end of the earth.'

Claire was also worried that Martin was getting too serious. She liked him as a friend but had no intention of settling down with him or anyone else yet. Most of her friends were either engaged, married or living with a partner and some even had children, but she didn't feel ready for that. Claire sometimes wished that she could be different.

'You're letting life pass you by,' one of her friends had said.

That was probably true Claire thought, but there was nothing she could do about it. She'd been in love once and knew she would never feel that way about anyone else.

Everything had gone wrong though and it was all her own fault. If she'd acted differently she would have been married to Adam, but she'd lost her chance. Her silly pride had got in the way. Adam had wanted to explain everything but she'd refused to listen. She'd regretted it ever since. It seemed a lifetime ago. Was it only five years? Why was she thinking about this now?

It must have been the music. She'd heard it in the car as she was driving to Martin's flat. The *Warsaw Concerto*, Adam's favourite piece of music. He was always making her listen to it. Now after all these years, she couldn't hear it without remembering Adam. She should have got over him by now. Would she ever? It was because of Adam that she'd taken this job at Greenhill, wasn't it? He'd driven her there once and she'd fallen in love with the town. But Martin was her boyfriend now so why was she still dwelling on the past?

She'd found it very tiring settling down into a new school. Then the day before, she'd had worrying news which had caused her a sleepless night.

'Wake up, Claire. Your coffee's ready.' Martin gently tapped her on the arm.

'Oh,' Claire jumped. 'I'm sorry going off to sleep like that.' She looked at her watch. 'You should have woken me up.'

'I didn't want to disturb you.'

'I didn't sleep very well last night.'

'Why? What's wrong? Was it because you were excited about coming back to see me?'

'Er . . . No.'

'That was supposed to be a joke, Claire.'

'Oh. Sorry. I'm still half asleep. I was looking forward to seeing you, Martin, but I had a bad night because of what happened at school yesterday.'

'Tell me about it.'

'We're going to have an Ofsted inspection. Can you believe it? I've only just got over the one I had at my previous school.'

'When?'

'Immediately after Christmas.'

'So why are you getting in a state about it now?'

'Yes, but it will be hanging over me. And I'll spend Christmas worrying about it. There'll be so much paperwork to deal with before then.'

'Forget about it, Claire. Let's enjoy the weekend.'

'I'll try, but I wasn't expecting that.'

'Can you please think of something other than school?' Martin snapped.

Claire kept quiet after that. She drank her coffee. Martin never understood. I used to be able to talk about it to Adam though, she reflected. But of course he was a teacher too. He might even be a headmaster by now and he's probably married as well. Stop thinking of Adam, she chided herself. You've managed all these years without him, concentrate on Martin.

'I've made you some fresh coffee,' he

was saying. 'Lunch will be ready soon.'

'You're so domesticated,' Claire smiled. 'You look after me really well.'

'I try to. What shall we do after lunch?'

'Let's go for a long walk. I need some exercise.'

'There's a good concert at the Barbican tonight. I'm sure I could get tickets for it, if you'd like that?' Martin stroked her glossy chestnut hair.

She pulled away. 'Not tonight. I don't want to get home late.'

'You've only just arrived and now you're talking about going home,' Martin said peevishly.

'I'm sorry. Maybe we could go another time, when I'm not feeling so stressed.'

'Look Claire, you know you can always stay here and I'll sleep on the sofa. Then you wouldn't have to worry about driving in the dark. Or book into the B&B down the road?'

'No, Martin. I want to go home. I've got a busy time coming up.'

'Still thinking about school,' Martin remarked bitterly. 'There's more to life than teaching.'

Claire thought, I know that, but do the inspectors? She remembered how upset some of the staff had been at her last school. One gave in her notice after more than twenty years of teaching because she had received a bad inspection report.

Then the first time she had looked in the newspaper at the job advertisements, she'd spotted the position at Greenhill Infants School. Claire felt this was too good an opportunity to miss. Maybe a fresh start was what she needed.

Then she'd met Martin. She liked him and they usually got on well together, except when she mentioned school. Being with him made her life more interesting, but she wasn't madly in love with him as she had been with Adam. Claire feared she would never feel that way again.

After lunch Claire helped Martin load the dishwasher. Then he said, 'I think you were right. A long walk would do us good. It's a lovely afternoon. How about strolling through St. James's park? We might even see the pelicans. Then we could go on to Hyde Park. How does that sound?'

'Lovely, just what I need.'

'Hooray! You've agreed to one of my suggestions for once.' Martin smiled.

* * *

A few days later when the children had gone home, Timothy Harding, a young teacher who had also recently started work at Greenhill walked into Claire's classroom.

'What bad luck!' he remarked.

'What do you mean?'

'The inspection, of course.'

'Oh that. Yes it's very bad luck. I had one at my previous school just before I left.'

'So did I.'

'I never dreamt I would have another so soon.'

'Neither did I. Er . . . Claire . . . I don't suppose you fancy going out for a drink tonight, do you?'

'Oh, I'm sorry, I can't,' she murmured trying in vain to think up a good excuse. She'd been aware that Tim seemed to be getting interested in her and didn't want to give him any encouragement. 'Er . . . my . . . my boyfriend wouldn't like it.' That was true, but it sounded feeble to her.

'I should have realised. All the best girls get snapped up quickly. But as you've never mentioned anyone before, and you don't wear a ring, I hoped you were free like me.'

'I'm not engaged if that's what you mean, but I have got a regular boyfriend. He's in London.'

'I'll leave you in peace then.' Tim hunched his shoulders and walked away.

Claire watched his athletic figure, thinking he shouldn't have much trouble finding a girlfriend with his rugged good looks. I'm surprised he hasn't one already. I guess he's rather shy.

Claire returned to her comfortable flat and relaxed after a hard day at school. It was on the outskirts of the town, close to open countryside, very different from her previous home in London. It wasn't luxurious like Martin's, but it suited her even though he called it poky. That was why she had to travel to his flat on Saturdays.

'I like my comforts,' he'd said.

Martin had expensive tastes. There was no lack of wealth in his family. He enjoyed having money and spending it. He was always generous with Claire, but didn't seem to understand that she had to be very careful with money. She was on her own.

There was no-one she could turn to if she was in financial difficulties. She knew Martin would help if necessary, but Claire made sure this would not happen. She'd always managed well even when she'd lived abroad.

A few weeks later as Claire was getting ready to go home from school, Sally, a young colleague, hurried into her classroom. 'I've just seen one of the inspectors,' she said excitedly. 'He's gorgeous.'

'You must be joking. How can an inspector be gorgeous?'

'This one is. He's tall, blond and has a wonderful smile.'

'Are you sure he's an inspector?'

'Yes. Tim told me he was.'

'What's he doing here?'

'He's having a meeting with Julia. Tim said they always visit the school in advance to talk to the head teacher.'

'That's right; but from your description he doesn't sound like an inspector.'

'He smiled at me, Claire. You should have seen him,' Sally murmured dreamily. 'I was rushing along the corridor as usual when I bumped into him. I apologised but he said it was his fault, and then he smiled. Oh, I think I'm going to enjoy this inspection.'

'Don't be silly. No-one could.'

'But you haven't seen him. When you do, you might change your mind.

'I won't. Besides, there'll be three other inspectors and this one might not even come into your classroom. Even if he does, you'll be too busy teaching to look at him. What was his name?'

'I've no idea. Tim couldn't remember either. The inspection mightn't be so bad, Claire. I know you've taught a lot longer than I have,' Sally shrugged, 'But this one may be different. At least we'll have someone good to look at.'

'There'll be so much to do we won't have time to notice what any of them look like,' Claire replied tartly.

The next few weeks passed quickly. Autumn turned to winter and preparations were made for Christmas.

At school Tim continued to be friendly towards Claire. One day he asked, 'How's your boyfriend? Are you still seeing him? I was going to say . . . '

'He's all right, thanks,' Claire interrupted, 'and yes we are still together. What were you going to say?'

'It doesn't matter.'

'Haven't you got a girlfriend, Tim?'

'Unfortunately, no,' he mumbled.

'I can't think why,' Claire said kindly. 'I would have thought a lot of girls would want to go out with you.'

'But not the one I want.'

'Why's that?'

'Because she . . . she's got a boyfriend,' he muttered.

'I'm . . . ' Claire paused, realisation dawning on her. 'I'm sorry Tim. Got to go.'

She hurried away feeling embarrassed, wishing she'd not had that conversation with him. She didn't want the complication of Tim pining for her. She'd find that too upsetting. Was this because she still had yearnings for her lost love even though she was now in another relationship? Claire was unsure of her feelings towards Martin. She genuinely liked him and usually they

15

got on well together except when they were discussing her job, but it seemed to her that the romance was lacking.

★　★　★

It was now nearly Christmas. Claire had broken up from school for the holiday. As she packed her suitcase she wondered if she was doing the right thing.

'Come and stay with my family,' Martin had said. 'You can't spend Christmas on your own.'

'I could go and visit my sister Elizabeth in Scotland,' Claire replied. 'I usually do.'

'Will she be upset if you don't stay with her?'

'No, probably not.'

'Well, that's settled then. It's time you were introduced to my parents. I can't imagine how awful it must be for you, having no relatives except for one sister,' Martin said putting his arm around Claire. 'I love being part of a large family. You'll get on really well with my three brothers. They all want to meet you.'

'What have you told them about me?'

'Lots.'

'Martin?'

'Not much really,' he smiled. 'Just that you're the most beautiful girl I've ever seen.'

'Stop, you're making me blush.'

Martin put his finger on her lips. 'Shush,' he said kissing her.

Claire pulled away blustering, 'They'll be disappointed when they see me because I don't live up to your description.'

'Of course they won't. They'll love you just like . . . '

Martin hesitated and Claire quickly butted in, 'That's enough. You're making me nervous.'

Now that Claire was packing, she was regretting giving in to Martin and wishing she was going to Scotland to stay with her sister and husband as she had for the past two Christmases, since their mother and father had been killed in that dreadful car accident in Cyprus. Both parents had been only children. Claire and Elizabeth's grandparents had died long ago, and there were no other relations.

Elizabeth was ten years older and had married a Scotsman nine years before, leaving London to live in Edinburgh. At the time Claire was training to be a teacher and the two sisters had gradually drifted apart, meeting infrequently until the death of their parents. After that Elizabeth suggested, 'Why don't you come and live in Scotland? We're all that's left of our family, so we ought to stick together.'

'But I like living in London,' Claire had replied. 'I'd miss it too much. I have friends there.' That was true. After returning from working abroad, Claire had been glad to live in London for a time until she saw the advertisement for a job in Greenhill.

Elizabeth was shocked when she learnt that Claire was moving away from London, two years after their parents' death. 'You'll never settle in the country,' she said. 'It will be too tame for you. I thought you loved London. What's brought about this change of heart?'

'It's time I taught in a different sort of area. It will be good experience for me. Greenhill's not too far away. I can still get to London at weekends if I want.'

'But why Greenhill, have you a special reason for choosing it?'

'No,' Claire lied.

When Claire informed Elizabeth that she was going to stay with Martin's family for Christmas, she was quite excited. 'You haven't mentioned him before. Tell me all about Martin.'

'He's a bank manager. We've been going out together for a few months.'

'He must be serious if you're meeting his family. What's he like? Did you meet him in Greenhill?'

'No. He lives in London. He's tall, dark haired, good looking and very nice, but we're just friends.'

'Oh, is that all? What a shame. Perhaps you'll be more than that after this holiday. Maybe you'll come back with an engagement ring.'

'I don't think that's likely.'

'Why? It's time you settled down, Claire.'

'I'm happy as I am.'

'So, why did you move away from London?'

'It was all arranged before I met Martin.'

'What a shame. You're not getting any younger, Claire. Don't leave it too late to find the right man.'

'I'm not yet thirty,' Claire groaned. 'You make me sound like an old woman. There's plenty of time, but as I said I'm quite happy at the moment.'

'You didn't say that when you got engaged to Adam. You never did explain why you broke it off so suddenly. What happened?'

'It's all in the past. More than five years ago,' Claire muttered. 'Don't bring that up again. I don't want to talk about it. Everything was different then.'

It had been. She was so young when she met Adam, only twenty-two. She'd fallen head over heels in love with him. For a time, life had been wonderful and she'd been living in a dream world.

When Adam proposed she was deliriously happy, but this was short-lived. A few weeks afterwards her whole life had been turned upside down. If she'd been older and wiser maybe she would have acted differently, given Adam another chance.

At least she might have listened to his explanations, but instead her pride was so badly wounded that she'd fled from him. Later she regretted her actions; tried to make amends, but by then there was nothing she could do.

Claire shuddered at the thought. She was relieved that Elizabeth was on the other end of the telephone and couldn't see her reactions. I must stop thinking about all this, Claire told herself. I've got to put it behind me. I have a new life now. It was just that so many things reminded her of Adam and of what she had lost.

'Well, have a good time,' her sister was saying. 'Tell me all about it when you come home.'

Claire hung up, promising to keep in touch, but Elizabeth's words were going round and round in her head. How serious was Martin? Did he envisage a long term relationship with her? He hadn't talked about marriage. He's been a bachelor so long, he's probably quite happy as he is, Claire decided. That's fine by me. I don't know if I will get married now. I missed my chance five years ago.

★ ★ ★

'Hello dear. I'm pleased to meet you at last. My son's told me so much about you.' Mrs James kissed Claire on the cheek and Martin's father shook her hand. 'Come and sit down. I'll make some coffee.'

Claire seated herself on the sofa next

to Martin. She looked around the huge room which was extravagantly furnished. It was Christmas Eve.

She'd parked her car outside Martin's flat in London and he had driven them to the other side of the capital where his parents lived in a large detached house. Although he had described his parents' home to her, she hadn't anticipated it being so lavish. 'You didn't tell me it was like a stately home,' she chided.

'It's not, but I agree it is very comfortable. I suppose my brothers and I were fortunate in having such a privileged upbringing.'

'You certainly were. It's nothing like the small semi-detached house I lived in with my sister and my parents.'

'Elizabeth didn't mind you coming here for Christmas, did she?'

'No, not at all.' Claire didn't want to go into the details of what her sister had said.

The next few days passed pleasantly. Martin was off work until after the New

Year, so Claire had agreed to stay for the whole of that period. They spent time with his family, dined out, attended a concert, visited museums and went to the cinema. Martin was generous and enjoyed spending his money on Claire, buying her lavish gifts and countless boxes of expensive chocolates, until she protested, 'Please don't buy me any more, I'll put on so much weight, none of my clothes will fit when I get home.'

'You've got a perfect figure. I'm sure you've no need to worry,' Martin replied. However, he stopped buying chocolates and presented Claire with beautiful bouquets of flowers instead, until his mother complained that they were running out of vases to put them in.

Martin's Christmas present to Claire had been a gold necklace with matching earrings. She wished she had purchased something more elaborate for him than a sweater.

Claire met Martin's brothers and

their wives and girlfriends. She got on well with all of them and also with his parents who treated her like a daughter.

After the New Year celebrations, on their last night together before Claire had to return to Greenhill, Martin booked a table at a very exclusive restaurant in the west end of London. Claire had purchased a new outfit for the occasion. It was a gold satin, calf length, fitted dress. She'd searched the shops and had found a pair of perfectly matched high heeled shoes to go with it.

When she was dressed ready to go out, Martin whistled and said, 'Wow! You look wonderful. I love that dress.'

'The necklace and earrings you gave me for Christmas are just perfect with it,' Claire told him.

'I'm glad they came in useful. All the other men in the restaurant will be envious of me,' Martin replied.

Claire laughed. 'You look very dashing yourself,' she answered. That was true. He did in his elegant navy suit and pristine white shirt. If only she could fall madly in love with him, then life would be so simple, but always at the back of her mind was the image of Adam, which no man could assuage.

Martin took Claire's hand and led her to his car, saying, 'This is going to be a night to remember.'

She felt uneasy about this remark and wondered why. After all, he'd been good to her this holiday. They'd had a lovely time and she'd enjoyed meeting his family. Everyone had made her feel very welcome.

So why was she uneasy? Just relax and enjoy the evening Claire told herself. You'll soon be back at school. There'll be no time for fun then. Only two weeks to go till the inspection.

'Wake up, Claire. We're nearly there.' Martin interrupted her daydreaming.

'I wasn't asleep. I was thinking.'

'What about?'

'The inspection. It won't be long now.'

'Oh Claire, please don't spoil the

evening by talking about school. Can't you forget it for a while?'

'Sorry. I won't mention it again, but have you remembered that I won't be able to see you for the next two weekends?'

'We'll see about that.'

'What do you mean? I told you weeks ago that I'd have to devote myself one hundred per cent to the inspection.'

'And I said you can't be expected to work twenty-four hours a day.'

'It's only for two weeks. It'll soon be over,' Claire tried to reassure him.

'That's enough,' Martin snapped. 'Let's change the subject.'

Claire kept quiet as he parked the car. Her career was something that he was never going to understand.

Martin helped her out of his car and they walked the short distance to the restaurant in silence.

He ushered her inside and Claire gasped at the lavish surroundings. 'This'll cost you a fortune.'

'Don't worry about that.' Martin had

calmed down. He took hold of Claire's hand and squeezed it, adding, 'You're worth it.'

Claire enjoyed the feel of the soft, luxurious carpet underneath her feet as they followed the waiter to their table by a window. As she sat down she looked round at the rich furnishings, the elegant flower arrangements which adorned the restaurant and the candles placed discreetly on each table, giving just the right amount of light for an intimate dinner.

The waiter brought them some drinks as they perused the menu. 'There's so much choice, I don't know what to have,' Claire murmured.

'Choose whatever you like,' Martin replied.

When they had finally made their selections they sat back, sipping their drinks. Claire began to enjoy herself and wondered why she had been so worried earlier.

The meal was sumptuous; the ambience exquisite; and Martin was charming;

an almost perfect evening Claire thought.

As they were drinking their coffee at the end of the meal, Martin reached for her hand saying, 'There's something I want to ask you.'

Claire pulled away quickly murmuring, 'Can you excuse me a minute while I go to the cloakroom?'

As she hurried off she was aware that Martin was gazing after her with a puzzled expression on his face. Just when I was thinking that this was a nearly perfect evening, Martin has to spoil it, she thought. What's he going to say? He's getting too serious. I don't want this. So why did you stay with his family for Christmas she asked herself? You've probably given him completely the wrong impression.

Claire refreshed her make-up, combed her hair, all the while debating with herself what she should do. She walked slowly back to Martin. 'This is a lovely restaurant,' she said brightly.

'Yes, it is. That's why I brought you

here. I want this to be a special evening.'

'It has been,' Claire answered quickly, looking down, as she fiddled with the strap of her handbag.

'Claire, look at me. I don't know why you suddenly find your handbag so fascinating. I want to ask you something.'

Hesitantly she raised her face. 'Yes Martin.'

He took hold of her hand. 'Claire . . . will . . . will you marry me?'

An Uncertain Future

'What . . . what did you say?' Claire asked aghast, scarcely believing the words she was hearing.

'I said . . . will you marry me?'

'Oh . . . I, er . . . '

'Just answer yes,' Martin urged, grabbing her hand. 'You look astounded. Surely you can't be that surprised? You must know how I feel about you.' He was staring at her waiting for a reply. 'Say something, please Claire. I haven't asked anything improper.'

She tried to regain her composure, telling herself, you half expected this was going to happen. You've got to give a reply, but what? How could she tell Martin that she couldn't marry him, because even after more than five years, she was still in love with someone else? Adam. Who was probably married, and had forgotten that Claire ever existed.

Instead she lied, 'You have surprised me, Martin.'

'So, what's your answer?'

'I . . . I . . . I'm sorry, but I'm not ready for marriage,' she stammered.

'Oh, Claire,' he murmured.

She looked at his crestfallen face and felt terrible. 'I don't want to hurt you, Martin, but agreeing to marry someone is a big commitment. I . . . I don't want to make a mistake.'

'Does that mean you aren't turning me down altogether?' Martin said with hope in his voice.

'I suppose so. We haven't known each other a year yet. We don't need to rush into anything.'

'So I was premature in asking you?'

'Yes.'

'All right. I'll accept that. Perhaps I should have waited, but I thought you felt the same way about me.'

What does he feel for me, Claire wondered? Martin's never actually said he loves me, but then he's not usually a very emotional person.

'Are you listening, Claire?' He was saying. 'We get on so well together. We'd be good for each other. Will you please think about my proposal?'

It's all rather clinical, Claire was thinking, like a business arrangement. So different from when Adam proposed. He'd kissed me passionately not caring who was looking. But then to be fair to Martin, wasn't she always telling him not to kiss her in public as she didn't want to make a show of it? He probably thinks I'll be embarrassed if he embraces me in a restaurant.

'Well, will you think about it, Claire?' Martin was asking.

'I will,' she promised.

'Don't keep me waiting too long though. I'd like to be married before I'm forty,' he tried to joke.

He's right she thought. Am I going to waste my whole life dreaming about someone I can't have? Why am I thinking about Adam now? I suppose it's because Martin is the first person I've really got involved with, in all those years since I finished with Adam. It's time I started a new life. Maybe I should say yes. I don't want to be on my own for ever. We could have a good life together. I'll think about what he said.

'I can see I've ruined the evening,' Martin was saying. 'I wanted tonight to be special.'

'It has been,' Claire answered quickly, forcing herself to concentrate on what he was saying. 'I promise I will think about your suggestion.' She wanted to reassure him. 'We've had a lovely time and I'm very flattered by your proposal. I'll let you know what my decision is as soon as I can.' She felt she had to appease him because she hadn't given the answer he was hoping for.

'Thank you, Claire.'

'Martin,' her conscience was pricking. She hadn't told him about Adam. 'I think there's something I ought to tell you.'

'That sounds serious.'

Claire gulped. 'I've been engaged before.'

'You've been engaged,' Martin repeated looking stunned. 'I . . . I'd no idea. What happened?'

'It's a long story,' Claire murmured, knowing she could only ever let him know part of it. How could she tell him that she was still mourning for what might have been? 'I was very young at the time and it . . . it didn't work out.'

'I'm sorry, Claire. Now I think I understand. That's why you don't want to rush into another engagement. Is that it?'

'Yes, that's right.' She was relieved that he was taking it so well. It was better that he didn't know the real reason why she was hesitating; that she hadn't got her former fiancé out of her heart.

'When did all this happen?'

'Five years ago.'

'That long? Has there been anyone else since?'

'No. What about you, Martin? Have

you anything to tell me as it seems to be confession time?' Claire was trying to lighten a tense situation.

'There's nothing to tell,' he answered briefly.

★   ★   ★

That night Claire lay in bed thinking about Martin's proposal. She couldn't help remembering how different her reactions had been the day Adam proposed.

She'd been twenty-two when she and Adam met. She'd just left college with her degree and teaching qualification. Feeling very nervous, her heart thudding, Claire arrived at an outer London school one September morning ready to start her chosen career. As she entered the building the first person she saw was Adam. She took one look at him and her heart raced even more and her legs turned to jelly.

'You must be Miss Robinson, our new teacher,' he said holding out his hand and smiling. 'I'm Adam Black. It's my job to help any newcomers and this year you're the only new member of staff. I believe you'll be taking a year one class. Is that right?'

'Yes . . . er, please call me Claire.' She gazed up at his six feet three inch frame which dwarfed her, noting his blond hair and the curl which he pushed away from his eye. Those eyes . . . green and vibrant, staring straight into hers!

'Don't look so worried, Claire. This is a lovely school. I'll show you round. We're all friendly, staff and children alike,' Adam reassured her. 'You'll be fine.'

And she was. Claire loved every minute she was in that school.

Adam went out of his way to offer help and guidance to her. She noted that he did the same to all members of staff. He was adored by the children and very popular with the other teachers. Claire had fallen for Adam the moment she set eyes upon him, but with his great charm and stunning looks she believed she had little chance of attracting him.

She was aware that several other female staff were interested in him. Claire felt like a schoolgirl in comparison. They were older and more sophisticated. In school Adam treated everyone equally, showing no preferences, having a caring and considerate manner to all.

One evening about a month after Claire had started teaching, as she was leaving school, Adam walked out of the building behind her. They started discussing their work, and then Adam said, 'Claire, I hope you don't mind me asking, but do you like classical music?'

Feeling curious about what was coming, she answered, 'Yes, very much.' Adam was in charge of music in the school and she guessed that he was going to ask her to help with one of his musical productions.

'Good. I . . . I've got tickets for a concert at the Festival Hall on Saturday and I wondered if you would like to come with me? That is, if you're not busy? It's Rachmaninov, his Second Piano Concerto.'

Claire could hardly believe her ears. She nearly danced with joy. Adam Black wanted to go out with her! 'I'd love to come and that's one of my favourite works,' she replied shyly.

That had been the beginning of their romance. Soon they were going out together regularly. Claire was amazed at her good fortune and wondered why Adam was interested in her when he could have had the pick of so many other women. They didn't tell any of the staff as Adam felt it was best to keep quiet about their relationship. She found it hard seeing him every day and having to act in a formal way when really she would have liked to rush up and kiss him.

A few weeks later, Adam said, 'I've applied for another job. I think it would be better if we worked in different schools. It's putting too much strain on us being together all the time.'

Claire felt disappointed that she wouldn't see Adam every day, but she understood his reasoning. He'd warned her that if the rest of the staff found out about them, they'd be the target for a great deal of gossip, and neither wanted that.

'We'll still see a lot of each other,' he assured her. 'Besides, it's time I thought about promotion.'

After their first Christmas together, Adam started work as a deputy head teacher at a primary school, still in the same part of London, but in a much tougher area.

At twenty-nine Adam was seven years older than Claire. He was ambitious, intending one day to become a head teacher. He had taught throughout the primary age group, working in several different schools to gain a variety of experiences. Claire, however, preferred teaching the youngest children.

Like Claire, Adam had been living at home with his parents, but when he secured his new post, he decided to purchase his own flat. She had gone with him helping to choose one not too far from where she was living with her family. He soon settled in and Claire often visited him there.

One day Adam suggested they went out for a drive. 'I want to show you something,' he told her.

After about an hour they stopped by a lake in a small town in the heart of the countryside. 'This is Greenhill,' he told Claire. 'I used to come here when I was a boy. My grandparents lived here. I've always loved the place.'

Claire was impressed too. It was a beautiful day and the sun was gleaming on the lake turning everything to gold. Swans were gliding across the water, birds were warbling, and bees were buzzing from one plant to the next collecting pollen. They walked along hand in hand. Claire thought that she would remember this day for the rest of her life. After they had completed their circuit of the lake, Adam led her towards a more built-up part of town. They came to a street of bungalows.

'Here it is,' he said at last, stopping outside a dilapidated one. 'Number twenty-seven. This was my grandparents' home. Oh, dear,' he sighed. 'It doesn't look the same. It's so neglected and dingy. When they lived here, there were masses of flowers in the front garden and my granddad was always giving the walls a fresh coat of paint.'

Claire nodded sympathetically. 'When you go back and revisit somewhere, it rarely seems as good as you remember.'

'If the bungalow was up for sale and I had enough money, I'd buy it and try to restore it to its former glory, but on my teacher's salary I couldn't afford to.' Adam's voice was tinged with regret.

'Maybe you'll be able to when you become a head teacher.'

'Perhaps, but the present owner may never want to sell.'

'Then, you'll have to keep visiting Greenhill to see if it ever does go up for sale.'

'I might do that,' Adam replied.

Claire had fallen in love with Greenhill too. It was a compact town, but it had all the essential services, a good shopping centre, several old and attractive churches, the country park with its lake, a library with a museum inside, a concert hall and a theatre. Claire had decided that she too would like to live there one day, but after she and Adam had split up, thought that would never happen, yet here she was living and working there.

Claire continued to toss and turn, sleep still eluding her. She couldn't escape from those memories of the past. Her parents had owned a holiday villa in Cyprus. It was while they were staying there that her mother had been taken very ill and as her father couldn't cope, Claire had felt compelled to leave Adam and resign from her job in London to go out to Cyprus to care for her mother.

At the same time she was fortunate enough in obtaining some supply work at a school for the British servicemen's children. She and Adam had kept in touch by telephone making plans to meet during the summer holiday. However, her mother recovered more quickly than they'd anticipated so her parents returned to England, leaving Claire still working in Cyprus. Then one weekend she made a surprise visit to England to see Adam. It was then that the stupid misunderstanding occurred which caused her to break off the engagement. She'd taken off her ring and sent it back to Adam by registered post and fled back to Cyprus. He'd telephoned demanding an explanation.

'What have I done?' he asked.

'Stop pretending,' she'd answered. 'You know very well what you've done.'

'I really don't know,' he insisted, but she didn't believe him and wouldn't listen to anything he said.

She'd acted hastily and regretted it ever since. Claire then decided to live in her parents' villa and was offered a job at the school where she had been a supply teacher. Adam had written and telephoned her frequently begging her to come back, but in a fit of rage she tore up his letters and ignored his phone calls

After a while, when Claire had calmed down a little, she thought she should have given him the opportunity of explaining his actions. Then his letters and phone calls stopped coming and she realised too late that her stubborn pride had got in the way and caused her to lose the love of her life. She wished with all her heart that she had behaved differently. She was determined to return to England and seek Adam out to see if there was any possibility of them being reconciled.

After some time, Claire managed to get a job at a school in London once more but she discovered that Adam was no longer living at his old address and his parents had moved too. As she was unable to trace him, Claire's secret hopes of being reunited with Adam now seemed impossible.

Three years later, whilst browsing through the *Times Educational Supplement* she saw the advertisement for a teaching post at Greenhill. She wanted a change from teaching in London so finally decided to have a go. When she was selected for the job, she was overjoyed. She'd often wondered if Adam had fulfilled his dream and gone to live in Greenhill.

She imagined meeting him there one day and discovering that he was living in his grandparents' bungalow. How silly you're being, she chided herself. That's a fairy story. Things like that don't happen in real life. She'd even gone to see the bungalow but found that it was still in a dilapidated state, much as it was when Adam had taken her there, so different from how he'd described it.

* * *

Claire left Martin in London and returned to Greenhill to get ready for the inspection. Two days later she received a telephone call from a former teaching colleague. They exchanged New Year greetings and then her friend said, 'You'll never guess what I heard.'

'You sound excited about something.'

'Well, I've found out what happened to Adam Black.'

Claire could feel her heart racing, but she tried to appear calm. 'What happened to him?'

'He got married and moved away from London.'

Claire's heart nearly stopped beating. Adam married! Her worst nightmare had come true.

'Did you hear me Claire? You've gone very quiet. Adam Black got married. Oh, you're not still hankering after him, are you?'

'No. Of course I'm not.' Claire pulled herself together. How did you find that out?'

'I met Lorraine at a party. She told me. Do you remember her?'

'Yes. We used to teach together years ago.'

'Well, apparently she kept in touch with Adam for some time after you broke up with him, but since his wedding she's heard no more.'

'How did you come to talk about Adam?'

'We were reminiscing about past times and people we used to teach with when she mentioned him.'

'Who did he marry?' Claire had to ask, even though she felt as if a knife was twisting inside her.

'No-one we knew. I'd often wondered what had happened to him after you'd gone abroad to teach. It was a shock to everyone, you leaving like that. We'd all thought you and Adam were made for each other.'

'Well, we weren't,' Claire interrupted, not wanting to hear any more

As soon as she'd finished the telephone call Claire burst into bitter tears. How ironic, that now she was living in Greenhill, she had to discover

Adam was married. Worse still, he could be living there too, and she might bump into him with his wife! What would she do then? Another awful possibility struck Claire. Children . . . Adam had always wanted children. What if he was a father? She couldn't bear to meet Adam out with his child. Her first thought was, I'll have to leave Greenhill. But I like it here, she reasoned.

My life with him was in the past. I've got to forget that. Now I know what happened, I can make a closure on that part of my life. I've my future to consider. Could it be with Martin?

For the next few days Claire was busy getting everything ready for the inspection. She had sleepless nights not only worrying about that, but also about what her reply to Martin should be. There was no-one she could turn to for advice. She alone had to make the decision. Martin would be good to her. She knew that, but was it the right basis for marriage?

He would send frequent text messages and emails as well as telephoning her. Whenever he asked how she was, Claire always replied, 'Fine.' Even though she was dreading the inspection, she made no reference to it, knowing that Martin had little understanding and sympathy for her feelings.

The night before it was due to start, he phoned her again. 'How are you, Claire? And don't just say, 'fine' this time, please. I know you're worried about tomorrow. You can tell me about it.'

'I didn't think you were very interested in my career, Martin.'

'I'm interested in every part of your life, Claire. You should know that. After all, you're the woman I want to marry. And while we're on that subject, have you thought any more about your answer?'

'I have.' That was true. She'd pondered over it every night until finally she'd made her decision.

'And have you come to any conclusion?'

'Yes.'

'I would make you happy,' Martin continued, seeming not to have heard Claire's reply. 'If we were married you could give up teaching. I earn enough to support us both. I know you like children and I'd be willing to start a family soon, if you wanted. Please say 'yes', Claire.'

'All right. I will.' She forced the words out. She couldn't go through life dreaming about her first love. She would forget Adam and devote herself to making Martin happy. She did love him in a way, although not passionately as she had Adam, but she cared for Martin and wanted the best for him. They would spend their lives together and she'd do everything she could to make a success of their marriage, and maybe one day this aching void in her would go away.

'You will? Is that what you said? Your voice was so quiet, I'm not sure if I heard right.'

'Yes Martin, I will marry you.'

Claire's voice was loud and strong now, full of resolution.

'Oh,' Martin gasped incredulously. 'I can't believe it. Thank you, Claire. You won't regret it. If we weren't on the telephone, I'd give you such a kiss. When can I see you again?'

'Saturday? That's not too far off.'

'I don't know if I can wait that long.'

'You'll have to,' Claire laughed, caught up in Martin's enthusiasm. 'My inspection will be over then and I'll feel like celebrating.'

'We will, with champagne. Once we're married you won't have to worry about any more inspections. Ring me up tomorrow and let me know how it's going. I'll be looking forward to hearing from you.'

Claire debated with herself whether to ring her sister to let her know she was going to marry Martin. She knew Elizabeth would be delighted, but didn't know if she could cope with the interrogation her sister was sure to give.

Earlier in the week, Claire had

telephoned Elizabeth and told her that she'd had a good Christmas, but that was all. After much deliberation she decided to inform her sister, guessing she would be upset if she thought Claire had kept it from her.

As anticipated, Elizabeth was thrilled, 'A wedding! Oh, I'm so pleased for you. I can't wait. When are you getting married? I hope it's in the summer. Where are you going to live? Has he bought you a ring?'

Claire was overwhelmed by her sister's interest and couldn't begin to answer her questions. A ring . . . she hadn't thought about that. She didn't want a diamond solitaire like the one Adam had bought. What did he do with it? Had he given it to his . . . his wife? He promised that he would keep it in case Claire changed her mind, but she'd told him not to.

'Give it to someone else,' she'd shouted over the telephone.

'I'll never do that,' he'd said, but maybe he had.

Stop torturing yourself about the past, Claire chided. It's the present you need to think about. Perhaps a sapphire ring would be better this time. She'd tell Martin that. Supposing he went out and bought one for her. What would she do if he gave her a solitaire? I'd just have to accept it, Claire decided.

'Are you still there?' Elizabeth was asking. 'You've gone very quiet. You haven't answered my questions.'

'I'm sorry. This is a terrible line. I couldn't hear you very well. What did you say?' Claire lied.

In the end, she told her sister that no plans had been made as they'd only just got engaged. This at least was true. She guessed that Martin would want to sort things out at the weekend. As soon as the inspection's over she'd put her mind to it and try to show some enthusiasm for her future life with Martin.

After promising Elizabeth that she'd keep her informed of all their plans, Claire hung up, wishing that she could feel as excited as her sister. For Martin's sake she'd have to try. After all, she'd agreed to marry him, so now he was the only man she should think about. Get Adam out of your system. Forget him, she told herself once more. But even as she thought this, memories of his proposal came flooding back.

They'd been going out together for about eighteen months. It was summer. The weather was sunny and warm. Adam had said, 'Let's spend tomorrow by the sea.'

Claire had risen early. She'd packed a picnic lunch. Adam drove them there in his car. They spent hours sunbathing, swimming and paddling in the sea, holding hands.

She had wished the day would last for ever. When at last it was time to leave the beach, Adam suggested, 'Why don't we take a walk along the promenade?'

Claire agreed eagerly, wanting to prolong the day. As they walked hand in hand, looking at the sea, sparkling in the evening sunshine, they were enveloped in their own world, oblivious of everyone around them. They reached the end of the promenade. A steep pathway led onto the cliffs. Adam helped Claire along the stony track until they reached the highest point. They both stopped and gasped at the amazing view.

'This is a wonderful place,' she breathed.

'It is,' Adam agreed. Then he turned towards Claire, pulled her into his arms and kissed her passionately. 'I love you. Will you marry me?'

She'd been so overcome by the whole experience that she nearly stumbled, but Adam's strong arms held her firmly. 'I love you too,' she whispered, 'And yes, I will marry you.'

He whooped with delight, lifting Claire off the ground, swinging her around, planting kisses all over her face and neck, until she was breathless and begged to be put down. They'd almost skipped back to the car like two carefree children, unconcerned by the amused looks they were getting from passers-by.

'It's a good thing none of our pupils can see us now,' Adam said and Claire had laughed happily.

A few days later Adam had gone out and bought Claire a beautiful diamond solitaire ring, presenting her with it when they went for a celebration meal.

'It's perfect, just what I would have chosen,' she told him.

For the next few weeks Claire's happiness was complete, until everything changed when she had to go to Cyprus to look after her mother who was sick.

Claire forced her mind back to the present, vowing that this would be the last time she would allow herself to indulge in thoughts of the past. Her life with Adam was over. There was nothing she could do to change that.

From now onwards, she would stop comparing the two men. Instead she would concentrate on making Martin happy, and maybe in doing that, she would become happy herself.

The next morning, Claire arrived at school early. She'd decided not to tell anyone of her engagement. They'd all have other things on their mind, she reasoned. Besides, she wanted to get used to the idea herself, before spreading the news around. Claire met Sally in the playground and they walked into the building together. 'I'm really dreading this,' Claire told her.

'So am I.'

'I thought you'd be looking forward to it,' Claire mocked.

'Why? What do you mean?'

'Well, you'll see the gorgeous inspector again, or have you gone off him already?'

'No, I'm still interested in him, but it's the others I don't want to see.'

'I don't want to see any of them,' Claire stated vehemently. Then it occurred to her that once she and Martin were married, she might give up teaching and wouldn't have to face this ordeal again. Now that would be something to look forward to.

'I suppose it'll soon pass. They'll only be coming into our classrooms on four days.' Sally was trying to sound positive.

'That's right. On Friday they'll be presenting their findings to Julia,' Claire agreed.

They walked into the staff room to look at the notice board to see if there were any important messages. Everywhere was neat, tidy and smelling of polish. Little vases of flowers adorned the shelves.

'It looks a bit different to usual in here,' someone commented.

'Yes. What a transformation! You'd think the Queen was coming. Not a bunch of miserable inspectors,' a young woman replied. 'There's a list up of their names if you're interested,' she added.

'I'm not, but I suppose I'd better look,' Claire muttered walking over to the board. She and Sally peered at it.

'The registered inspector's a Mr

Black,' Sally commented, laughing. 'I knew it was a colour. I kept thinking it was a Mr Green.'

Claire's heart missed a beat. She read the notice again. The team of four inspectors was headed by a Mr A Black. What a terrible coincidence, she thought. Just when I'd resolved to stop thinking about Adam, I discover that our chief inspector not only has the same surname as him, but his first name starts with the same letter too. I wonder what the A stands for, maybe Albert or Alfred or even Arthur.

They're good old names suitable for an elderly inspector. Then she remembered that Sally had said he wasn't elderly. In fact, she thought he was young and gorgeous. So perhaps his name was Alex or Andrew. What does it matter? Claire asked herself. Stop fussing over the inspector's name. It's not important.

'Good luck,' she called to Sally as they hurried to their classrooms.

Even if this is going to be the last

inspection before my marriage, I want to do well, Claire thought as she busied herself ready for the day ahead. Better to go out in a blaze of glory, than to slink off under a cloud. You're being a bit dramatic today, she told herself. It must be the combined effect of getting engaged and the inspection.

She re-read her lesson plans, trying to anticipate all eventualities, knowing that young children often said and did surprising things when another adult entered the classroom. If that happened all her plans could be thrown off course.

The first part of the day went well. Claire had warned her class to be on their best behaviour. She had told them that visitors were coming to see if they were being good. At playtime she reported to Sally that no inspector had been anywhere near her classroom. Several other members of staff were bemoaning the fact that they had been visited, but no-one had seen the registered inspector.

'He's with the Head,' Tim told them. 'He arrived at eight o'clock this morning, carrying piles of folders. I saw Julia smile sweetly at him and they've been ensconced together ever since.'

'Discussing all of us,' I suppose,' Sally remarked.

'I guess so, and the general running of the school,' someone added. 'He'll soon be coming to see us. We won't escape.'

At lunchtime Sally burst into the staffroom excitedly. She'd been visited twice. Once by a woman inspector and the other time by Mr Black. 'I was so nervous,' she confided, 'but he told me not to worry.'

'Just carry on as usual,' he said.

'I tried to, but it was difficult with such an Adonis there. I found it hard to concentrate. Afterwards he smiled and I went quite weak at the knees. I think he was pleased with everything though.'

'You sound as if you've made a hit there,' Tim teased.

'You've got to admit, he doesn't look

like the average inspector,' another young member of staff added.

'What does an average inspector look like?' Tim asked.

'I don't know, but this one's very dishy.'

'Let's hope he gives us all a good report then,' Tim replied. 'You might change your mind about him if he doesn't. What was the woman like?'

'Fine,' Sally answered.

'I still haven't seen anyone,' Claire wailed. 'I expect someone will come this afternoon when I'm in the hall. I've got P.E. first. I'd prefer it if they didn't come then, especially when the children go back into the classroom to get organised. That's always a chaotic time.'

Claire was right. The lady inspector came in to watch her P.E. lesson. The children behaved impeccably, getting out and putting away the apparatus with the minimum of fuss. As the inspector left the hall, Claire breathed a sigh of relief. She felt proud of her class and could have hugged them all.

The children had just returned to their room and were getting organised when the door opened. Claire didn't hear it because of the general hubbub of children chatting and milling around. Some were waiting for her help. She was bending over tying up someone's shoelaces and didn't see the very tall, blond figure walk in.

'There's a man in our room, Miss Robinson,' a little boy called.

Before she could look up, she heard a deep voice saying, 'Don't take any notice of me, Miss Robinson. Just carry on with what you're doing.'

Claire fumbled with the shoelace, thinking what's the matter with me? I must be imagining things now. That voice . . . it sounds like . . . No, it can't be. She straightened herself, turned round and looked up into the eyes of Adam Black who was staring down at her.

The Past Returns

Claire heard Adam's sharp intake of breath as he murmured, '*You?*' The smile faded from his face, disbelief taking over. However, after a few moments, seeing the group of children observing them, he quickly regained his composure, saying, 'Miss Robinson, I'll sit in the corner so I won't be in your way.'

'Er, yes, Mr Black.' Claire felt as if she were dreaming. This couldn't really be happening. It was a nightmare and she would wake up soon.

'Miss Robinson, I've got my laces in a knot. Will you help me please?' One of Claire's pupils was tugging impatiently at her skirt.

'Oh . . . I'm sorry, Billy. Let me see.'

Claire tried to carry on as normal, but she couldn't ignore the huge man sitting squashed up on a tiny chair in the corner of the classroom. Her sense of unease seemed to be conveyed to the pupils and they became unruly and wouldn't settle down to finish the work which had been left on their tables. The noise in the room became louder and louder as children chatted and bickered with each other, few actually attempting to do any work in spite of Claire's desperate pleas for them to be quiet.

She longed for Adam to go, but he didn't. He sat there, referring to her lesson plans, looking round at the children and writing copious notes. She realised that her pupils were not going to produce any worthwhile work if they carried on in the same manner so she said, 'Boys and girls, please pack your work away quietly. We'll do some singing and if you're very good, I might let you play the percussion instruments.'

Claire could see Adam staring at her. She was hot and bothered, her face was flushed and she felt as if she were on fire.

A small cheer went round the classroom. Claire held up her hand and the children quietened down at once. Soon they were all sitting cross-legged on the floor in a circle around their teacher. A large container full of percussion instruments was placed in the middle. The unruly atmosphere was gone and all were co-operating with each other to produce music.

One little boy called out to Adam, 'Do you want to join in?'

Claire quickly chided him. 'Don't disturb Mr Black, please Jason. He's busy.'

'It's all right, Miss Robinson. Jason's not bothering me.' Then turning to the child, he said, 'Thank you for asking me, but I've got some writing to do. I'll just watch instead.'

The rest of the afternoon progressed well. The children listened carefully to the story Claire told them, and afterwards they were able to answer correctly all the questions which she posed.

Shortly before the bell rang for the end of afternoon school, Adam walked to the door and said, 'I'll come back to your room in about half-an-hour if I may, to give you feedback from your lessons?'

'Yes, that should be all right,' she assured him, I'm seeing Miss Jarrold in about ten minutes.'

'Good. I'll see you then.'

Claire felt relieved that he was going, but was still in a daze from seeing him again. Once the children had gone home she hurried to the staff room to fetch a glass of water before her interviews with the inspectors. She met Tim on the way. 'How did it go?' he asked. 'Did you have anyone in this afternoon, Claire?'

'Yes. Two.'

'So did I, it wasn't too bad though. How did you get on?'

'Sorry, I can't talk now, Tim. I've got to go back and have a chat with Miss Jarrold first and then . . . Mr, er, Black.'

'I've got two interviews as well. We'll

commiserate with each other another time, but you'll be OK with Mr Black. He's very nice, so I'm told. Not like the usual inspectors.' Tim comforted her.

'I hope so,' Claire muttered as she returned to her room, trying not to spill the water on the way. Her head was in a whirl. Adam's an Ofsted inspector! She'd never envisaged that in all her wildest imaginings. Even after seeing his name on the list this morning, she still hadn't suspected it was him.

Whatever possessed Adam to become an inspector? When they'd been going out together, he'd never even hinted that he wanted to be one, although he had always intended trying to become a head teacher. Like her, Adam had not held a good opinion of inspectors. Something drastic must have happened to make him change his mind. Was it the influence of his wife? Whatever it was, I'll never be able to ask him about it, Claire mused.

She quickly started tidying her room. A few minutes later, Miss Jarrold came in and gave some very good feedback from her P.E. lesson.

'You did really well,' she ended up saying. 'The children enjoyed themselves and worked hard, co-operating with each other in getting out and putting the apparatus away. You had great control of the class.'

Claire felt pleased and very relieved. At least I've got one good report she thought. She dreaded seeing Adam again and was concerned that her interview with him would not go so well. What would he say about her disastrous lesson? Even though she'd quickly contained any unruly behaviour, he'd probably criticise her for it. She had no time for further speculation. There was a knock on the classroom door and she saw Adam standing there.

'May I come in?' he asked.

'Of course.' Claire ushered him towards her table. 'You can sit here. I've cleared a space.' She was trying to sound business like and professional, but she could feel her heart hammering and her knees were trembling.

'Are you sure you'll be all right there?' Adam asked as she sat down on one of her pupil's tiny chairs.

'Yes, I'm used to it, thanks.'

'I won't keep you long, but I need to talk to you about your performance today.'

Claire blushed and averted her eyes.

'It was a shock meeting you today. I had no idea you were back in England and teaching in Greenhill,' Adam told her. His voice was clipped and expressionless as if he were trying to eradicate any traces of emotion.

Claire looked up and saw him staring at her left hand. 'It was probably even more of a shock for me,' she retorted, trying to stop herself from shaking. 'I knew one of the inspectors was a Mr Black, but I never dreamt it was you.'

Claire wanted to say, whatever happened to make you decide to become an inspector? But she thought that would not be very wise. After all,

71

he was here to write a report on her. She didn't want an adverse one, even though her teaching career would soon be cut short when she married Martin.

'This is all rather embarrassing, Claire.' Adam flushed and looked away. 'I don't think we should let anyone know that we know each other.'

'No, I suppose not. It would be difficult for you, having to say to the Head and the school governors, by the way, one of the staff, Miss Robinson, used to be my fiancée.'

'Quite.' Adam clenched and unclenched his hands, still not looking at Claire.

'I won't say anything.'

'Thank you. Now we've dealt with that matter, we'll get back to business.' Adam's tone was brusque.

Claire couldn't quite beieve it. Where's the old Adam gone? He would never have acted like this. But five years have gone past, she told herself. You're both grown-up now. What did you expect Adam to do? Sweep you into his arms and kiss you passionately? That's not going to happen. He's a married man and you're engaged to someone else.

Claire was brought back to reality by Adam saying, 'I'm sorry I walked into your room at an inopportune moment, when the children were sorting themselves out after P.E., I realise that is not an ideal situation to be observed, but you handled it well.'

'Thank you,' she glanced up, seeing Adam properly for the first time since he had walked into her classroom. His blond hair was shorter than she remembered and had a tinge of grey at the sides. There were faint lines around his eyes, but this just made him appear distinguished. He was still incredibly handsome. Then Claire's eyes focussed on the ring gleaming on the fourth finger of Adam's left hand. She tried to concentrate on what he was saying about her teaching, but she couldn't stop her mind from wandering.

She was shocked when she heard, 'You deviated from your lesson plans this afternoon. Can you tell me why?'

That was obvious to anyone, Claire thought, but decided she'd better not say that. She'd give him an honest answer though. 'After P.E. I could see the children were unsettled. I knew it was pointless expecting them to complete the work on their tables. They wouldn't have done it properly, so it seemed more sensible to do something else.'

'Something you knew you were good at? Trying to impress me, were you? Music was always your best subject and you knew it was my speciality too.' Adam stared at her arrogantly.

'No, I was not.' Claire's face had reddened with anger. He was deliberately provoking her, but she was in no position to defend herself. She was at his mercy. What could she say?

'You've made it difficult for me,' Adam went on. 'I have to write in my report how well you followed your lesson plans, but you suddenly changed mid-way.'

Claire glared at Adam. *He thinks I've made it difficult for him. He's made it impossible for me! What has happened to him? He would never have acted like this before.*

'Well, were you trying to impress me?' His voice was impatient.

'Certainly not,' Claire snapped. 'I'm sorry if I've caused you any bother. That was not intended. At the time I believed I was doing the right thing in changing my lesson plans. And given the same circumstances I would do it again.'

'Thank you for clarifying the situation. We'll say no more about it. Instead we'll talk about what actually went on in your room this afternoon.'

What an ordeal, Claire was thinking. *He's giving me a really hard time.*

They went on to discuss other aspects of her teaching and she was relieved that after a bad start, Adam made no other adverse criticisms and even gave her a few compliments. Gradually he seemed to become more relaxed and this made Claire feel less nervous.

Overall she decided that he had given her a fair report and was grateful for this. He had become completely professional. Claire thought that if anyone had walked into her room, they would have been unaware of the tension there had been between them. She felt proud of her controlled performance, thinking no-one would believe that Adam was her former fiancé.

When the interview was over, he shook Claire's hand murmuring, 'I never thought I'd see you again . . . and here in Greenhill. I can't believe it.' Then he walked out of the classroom.

Claire sat down trying to catch her breath, feeling shattered by the experience. Being inspected was bad enough, but finding out that the chief inspector was your ex-fiancé was unbelievable. She wished she could go straight home, but instead had to get everything prepared for the next day. She felt weak and her limbs were shaking. Claire wondered how she was going to get through the rest of the week. She made a supreme effort and started tidying up and getting out all the equipment she would need for the next day.

Suddenly Sally flew into Claire's room. 'I've been dying to talk to you,' she said. 'I saw Mr Black come out some time ago. How did it go?'

'Not too bad.'

'He's dishy, isn't he? Now do you understand what I meant about him?'

'Yes,' Claire answered quickly, not wanting to get into a conversation about Adam.

'It's hard to concentrate on your teaching when someone so gorgeous is in your classroom,' Sally said dreamily.

She's right, Claire thought. It was hard teaching in front of him, but not for the same reason. I didn't see the wonderful smile Sally keeps on about. In fact, I've never seen Adam so serious. It must have been as much a shock for him finding me here as it was for me discovering that he was our chief inspector. I wonder if he remembers taking me to Greenhill.

'Claire, you're not listening.'

Sally prattled on and Claire found it hard to be patient with her. She just wanted to get away from it all. Images of Adam past and present kept flashing through her mind. She remembered the way he'd once looked at her with love in his eyes, but today he'd glared; his face hard and cold. What else could you expect from an inspector, she asked herself? He was only doing his job.

'Look Sally, I can't talk now. I've got a headache. I'm going home.' Claire grabbed her bag, hastily throwing a pile of books inside, and started to walk off.

'I'm sorry,' her friend mumbled.

Claire glanced back and saw Sally watching, a hurt expression on her face. She felt mean for upsetting her, but she couldn't take any more today. She'd had enough. She drove home wishing she didn't have to go back the next day.

When she got in she slumped into an armchair, feeling too tired to prepare a meal. All the events of the day were mulling round in her mind. Could she telephone her Head and say she wasn't well? No, that wouldn't be honest and she'd have a guilty conscience.

It seems I'm destined not to forget Adam, Claire thought. Just when I'd resolved to get him out of my system, he has to turn up in Greenhill. But then a little voice in her head said, isn't that why you came to Greenhill in the first place, because you thought he might be there? Not even in her wildest nightmares had she imagined meeting him under these circumstances though. Adam's changed beyond belief, Claire decided. He was never pompous before. It must be the job. Maybe he thinks I've changed too. I probably have.

She was startled by her mobile ringing.

'How's the inspection going?' Martin asked.

'It's a bit gruelling. I'll be glad when it's over.' That's an understatement, Claire thought. She didn't dare tell him that the chief inspector was her former fiancé. What would Martin have to say about that?

'Once we're married, you'll be able to give up teaching, and devote yourself to looking after me,' he joked.

How thrilling does that sound? Claire thought mournfully. Then she felt annoyed with herself. He was only trying to help.

'It'll be a lot easier for you,' Martin continued.

'Will it?'

'Of course, I'm easy to look after.'

'I hope so,' Claire answered willing herself to feel more enthusiastic about her impending marriage.

'Oh, Claire. You sound so miserable.'

'I'll get over it. Don't worry about me. Once this inspection's over, I'll be back to normal.'

Would she ever be, Claire wondered? Was she doing the right thing agreeing to marry Martin? When she'd heard his voice her heart hadn't missed a beat as it did when she saw Adam. But you have a comfortable relationship with Martin, she thought. Why had Martin never married before now? He wasn't very forthcoming when she'd asked him if he had anything to confess. Did he have some skeletons in his cupboard?

'Are you still there?' Martin was asking. 'You're very quiet tonight.'

'Yes. I'm here. I'm just very tired.'

'I telephoned my mother last night. She and my father are delighted about our news. She wants us both to go and stay there one weekend, to discuss our wedding arrangements. Can we fix a date?'

'It will be nice to go and stay with them.' Claire tried to sound enthusiastic. 'But Martin, we haven't made any plans yet. We've only just got engaged.'

'Then it's time we did make some.'

'There's no rush. Let's just enjoy being engaged first. We can sort out a date to visit your parents at the weekend.'

'Did you tell your sister?'
'Yes.'

'What did she say?'

'She was very pleased.'

'What did the teachers at your school say?'

'I didn't tell them, Martin.'

'Why not?' He sounded disappointed.

'It isn't a good time at the moment, with everyone worried about the inspection.'

'I should have thought you'd be bursting to tell everyone. After all, it isn't every day you get engaged. But of course, I keep forgetting, you've done it once before. That's why you're so blasé about it.'

Claire could hear resentment in his voice. She was sorry she'd disappointed him, but she wasn't going to change her mind. At least she'd told Martin about her previous engagement, but he hadn't confided in her about any of his past relationships.

Claire was quite relieved when he eventually rang off. She spent the rest of the evening worrying about the inspection and whether she'd done the right thing in promising to marry Martin.

The next morning as Claire walked into school, Tim was the first person she met. 'Hello. Are you feeling better?' he enquired.

'I'm all right. I haven't been ill. What makes you think I have?'

'Sally told me you rushed home last night because you weren't feeling well. She said you seemed most peculiar.'

'Thanks,' Claire smiled. 'I hope I don't look peculiar now.' She thought Sally was right though. I did feel very strange after seeing Adam again.

'No. You look your normal charming self.'

'Good.' Claire had made a special effort with her make up to hide the ravages of her sleepless night. It had obviously worked. 'I only had a headache.'

'That Mr Black's nice, isn't he?' Tim continued. 'I'm glad he's the chief inspector. One of the other men is a bit prickly. Lucy was quite upset by him. He told her off for not sticking closely to her lesson plans.'

'That's what . . . A . . . er, Mr Black said to me.'

Tim gave her a sharp look. 'He told you off?'

'Sort of.' Claire wished she'd kept quiet.

'I'm surprised. Everyone has said how fair he's been.'

'It was my own fault. I did deviate from my plans.'

'I suppose that's what they're focussing on, whether we stick to our plans, come what may. But sometimes things happen which make it difficult.'

'I agree,' Claire said with feeling. 'And sometimes it's better to do something completely different. But inspectors can be very petty. Anyway, good luck, Tim. I'd better go and get ready for the fray.'

That day Claire was only observed once by one of the other inspectors. Everything went well and her interview with him was not the ordeal it had been with Adam.

Sally remained full of praise for Adam and seemed surprised that Claire didn't share her enthusiasm. Most of the other members of staff were also impressed and felt that he was giving them a fair report. I seem to be the only person who's been given a hard time by him, Claire thought. I suppose it was the shock of seeing me again that made him react badly.

Later that week, Martin rang and suggested they went out to buy the engagement ring on Saturday. Claire was pleased that she would be able to choose it herself. She would make sure it was totally different from her previous one. 'When I've placed it on your finger, we'll go to the Barbican. There's a good concert on.'

'That will be lovely, and for once as it's a special occasion, I'll not mind having a late night and driving back to Greenhill in the early hours of the morning.'

'Next week they'll all get a surprise when they see your engagement ring,' Martin said.

'I won't wear it for school. It would get spoilt. All that sand and water, not to mention plasticine and paint,' Claire apologised.

'But you will tell them we're engaged?' Martin urged.

'All right, but I don't know why you're so bothered about it.'

'I want everyone to know that you've agreed to become my wife.'

Claire couldn't argue with that.

That night she lay awake thinking about the inspection and her conversation with Martin. Then she remembered seeing the ring on Adam's finger. She'd hoped her friend had been wrong when she told her that he had a wife, but she wasn't. Why concern yourself with this now, she chided? You're engaged and Adam is married. Good! Soon the inspection will be over and you'll never see him again. Now it's time for you to settle

down with Martin and forget about
Adam, but could she do this?

* * *

The last day of the inspection came.
Claire had only caught glimpses of
Adam in passing, but there'd been no
exchanges between them.

She'd received good reports from the
other inspectors who had observed her
teaching and she was beginning to feel
that the worst was behind her.

'It'll soon be over,' Tim said.

'Thank goodness for that,' Claire
replied.

'Of course I'm glad the inspection's
nearly over, but I'll miss seeing Adam
around.' Sally joined in.

'Adam?' Tim enquired. 'Who's that?'

'Er . . . Mr Black.'

'Sounds as if you're getting very
friendly with him,' Tim teased.

'Don't be silly. I heard Julia calling
him that. It makes a change having a
really dishy man in the school. That's

the trouble with infant schools, they're full of women.'

'Thanks. What about me? Don't I count? I'm not a woman.'

'Sorry, Tim. I'm glad you're on the staff but . . . '

'I'm not dishy. That's what you mean.'

'No, you're very nice, but . . . '

'I'm not a dreamboat like Mr Black,' Tim laughed. 'OK Sally, I know that.'

'You're keeping very quiet, Claire. You could have helped me out. Have you noticed Adam's eyes?' Sally asked. 'They're so sad, even when he smiles.'

'I can't say I have.'

'I think he's hiding some dark secret. I know he wears a wedding ring, but maybe his wife doesn't understand him.'

'Yes, she probably can't forgive him for becoming an Ofsted inspector,' Claire blurted out bitterly, immediately regretting it, when she saw the others staring at her.

'You two certainly have vivid imaginations,' Tim replied. 'Inspectors have to be serious. 'It's their job. They can't keep making jokes.'

'I suppose you're right,' Sally agreed.

About half-an-hour before lunch time, Adam walked into Claire's classroom. She was in the middle of the daily literacy hour. She'd read a story and the children were doing work related to it. She was going round the room helping groups of pupils. She was so engrossed in her work that she didn't hear the door open. Suddenly she was aware of a shadow looming over her.

'Good morning, Miss Robinson. I won't stay long. I'll try not to get in your way.'

Claire's heart was racing and she prayed that everything would go well.

Adam went around questioning the children about their work. She was pleased that they were polite, well behaved and friendly towards visitors. As they were getting ready for lunch, he went to the door, saying he'd be back in a few minutes to speak to her.

This will be the last conversation I'll

ever have with Adam, she mused. I wonder if he's thinking the same thing. Why should he, she chided herself? You mean nothing to him now.

When he returned to her room, he told her that she'd done very well and would be receiving a good report.

'Thank you,' she replied, gazing into his eyes. Sally's right she thought. He does look sad. I wonder why. What's happened to him in all those years since we were engaged? He's a married man. He shouldn't be sad. He's still incredibly handsome though.

Adam took hold of Claire's hand and spoke quietly. 'I haven't yet recovered from the shock of seeing you here,' he murmured. 'You look just the same as I remember.'

'I think I must have aged after five years.' She tried to lighten the situation. 'At least I should be more sensible and mature.'

He ignored her remark and continued, 'We need to talk, but not here. Someone might come in. I'll be in touch. It won't be for some time, until all of this is completely over. Can I ring you? I'll find out your number.'

Claire didn't know what to reply, but she knew they couldn't stand there like that for much longer. Adam was right. Someone might come in. 'Yes, she nodded. I . . . I'll expect to hear from you in a few weeks.'

He let go of her hand, gave a slight smile and walked out of the classroom.

A Battle Of Wills

When Adam left her room, Claire asked herself, why ever did you agree to him getting in touch? You should have said, 'no'. But then you wouldn't have found out what he had to say, she thought. Will he tell his wife that he's going to ring you? Does she know that you were engaged to Adam? There were so many questions she wanted answered.

That afternoon Claire felt as if she were teaching in a trance. She was very relieved that no other inspectors entered the room. Her thoughts were continually of Adam, making it hard to concentrate on what she was doing. She was glad when the bell rang at the end of the school day.

Sally came hurrying into Claire's room, a broad grin on her face. 'I've just bumped into Adam Black,' she said. 'He was going into Julia's office. I dropped a pile of books in front of him and he picked them up for me.'

'You dropped them on purpose?' Claire asked incredulously.

'Of course not, I had too many and they just fell out of my arms. Adam rushed to retrieve them for me.'

He always was a gentleman, Claire thought.

'As he handed them over, he gave me one of his gorgeous smiles and said 'goodbye'. I told you the inspection wouldn't be too bad,' Sally went on.

'Well, I'm glad it's over,' Claire replied. 'Now we can get back to normal.'

'It's a shame we'll never see Adam again though,' Sally sighed.

'You may see him in a few weeks when he comes back with the final report or maybe even tomorrow. He's got to have a meeting with Julia to give her feedback from our inspection,' Claire told Sally.

'We have to make an action plan, don't we?'

'That's right. Then the inspectors have to study it, so they'll be back a few more times yet, unfortunately.'

'Let's hope it will be Adam who comes and not one of the others,' Sally answered.

'It will be A . . . Mr Black. He's the chief one. I don't know whether the others will return.'

'Good. I've just remembered, Tim wanted me to ask if you would like to come out for a drink tonight, to celebrate the end of the inspection?'

'Who's going?'

'About six of us, Jenny, Gina, Lucy . . . you know, the usual crowd.'

Claire didn't really feel like it but decided that perhaps she should. It would at least prevent her from dwelling on her encounter with Adam. 'All right,' she replied. 'But I don't want to be too late. You haven't forgotten that it is only Thursday. We still have to come to school in the morning.'

'I know, but we can be more relaxed tomorrow.'

Before going out that evening, Claire made a brief call to Martin, telling him that she was having a drink with some friends from school, but she was looking forward to seeing him on Saturday.

'Come as early as you can,' he begged. 'I can't wait to see you.'

Claire promised to do that.

She met Sally outside the Red Lion Inn at eight o'clock. They walked inside where the other young teachers were gathered together, laughing and joking in a carefree fashion.

'You lot certainly look a lot happier than you did on Monday,' Sally remarked.

'We are, aren't you?' Lucy asked.

'I suppose so,' Sally replied hesitantly.

'What's wrong with her?' Gina a young brunette wanted to know.

'She's still thinking about Mr Black,' Tim laughed. 'He's her dream man.'

'Well he is rather dishy,' Gina conceded.

'Can I get you two a drink?' Tim enquired of Claire and Sally.

A few minutes later he returned with two glasses. 'What have you been talking about? You're not still discussing the inspection, are you?' He asked as he heard the girls' chatter.

'Sally was just saying that all the best men seem to be taken.'

I second that, Claire thought.

'You're keeping very quiet over there, Claire,' Tim said.

'I'm listening to all of you,' she replied.

'OK,' Tim answered. 'Cheer up, Sally. There are plenty of other attractive men around.'

'Yes and you're looking at one right now,' Gina said pointing to Tim, who burst into fits of laughter.

'I wasn't referring to myself, but thanks Gina for the compliment,' he said bowing.

Sally seemed not to have heard them. 'They don't compare with Adam Black though,' she murmured.

No they don't, Claire echoed in her head.

After that they changed the subject and the inspection wasn't mentioned any more. The young people chatted, ate crisps and had a few drinks.

'We'd better go,' Lucy said. 'We don't want to be late for school in the morning.'

'Our taxi's arrived,' Jenny called to Gina and Lucy. 'See you all in the morning.' They hurried outside leaving Claire, Sally and Tim together.

'I'll escort you two home. It won't take long to walk. The fresh air will do us good,' Tim suggested to Claire. 'Sally, you don't look too well.'

'I really don't feel well.' Sally's colour wasn't good.

Claire took her other arm as they helped her out. It looked like something she'd eaten had disagreed with her.

'We'll soon get you home,' Tim assured her. 'You'll feel better after a good night's sleep.'

Claire was very relieved when they

arrived at Sally's flat. By now she was chalk white and holding her stomach.

'Can you find her key?' Tim asked.

Claire fumbled in Sally's bag, found the key and opened the door. He picked Sally up and carried her to the bedroom. She was a tall girl and Claire was amazed at how easily Tim was able to lift her. He gently placed her on the bed, making sure she was on her side, and then covered her with a blanket,

'Sally should be all right in the morning,' he told Claire. 'I think it must be something she ate.'

They stood watching as she slept, oblivious of their presence.

'You're so kind-hearted, Tim. You'll make someone a good husband one day.' Claire blurted the words out without thinking, then immediately regretted them.

'Thank you, but I don't think that's very likely now, do you?' He looked straight into her eyes and Claire had to avert hers, feeling embarrassed.

'There are a lot of nice girls around.

I'm sure you'll find someone soon,' she muttered.

'I'm not going to answer that,' Tim replied. Then changing the subject said, 'I'm worried about leaving Sally on her own. Someone needs to be with her. She might be ill in the night. I could sleep on the sofa and keep an eye on her.'

'You're right, but I should stay with her. She is my friend after all.'

'No. I'll call a taxi for you. It's better I stay. I don't think you could manage on your own. She's quite a big girl and you're so tiny.'

'How about both of us staying with her?' Claire suggested.

'If you're sure you don't mind. That would be better.' Tim looked at Claire gratefully. 'I'll make up a bed for you on the floor in Sally's room. I can take the cushions off the sofa. I'll sleep in the lounge in an armchair.'

Claire was thinking how kind and considerate Tim was. She had under-estimated him before. He was a much nicer person than she had realised.

* * *

During the night, Claire found it impossible to sleep. She felt on edge, listening in case her friend needed her. She thought back over the events of the past few days and hours. She decided that she wouldn't tell Martin about her staying the night in Sally's flat. He might misconstrue things, not understanding that she and Tim were there, only because her friend was ill.

She also kept thinking about her conversation with Adam. Would he ring her in a few weeks, or did he just say that? If he did telephone her, what was there to say? He'd said they needed to talk, but it was too late for that. He was married to someone else and she was engaged to Martin. What good could come from his phone call? It would have been better if they'd severed all connections then. This was just prolonging the agony.

At six o'clock Claire could hear Tim moving around. She decided to go home and change into something more suitable for school. She tapped on the lounge door and Tim opened it immediately.

'That's a good idea,' he replied when she told him her plans. 'If you stay with Sally now, I'll walk back to my flat and get the car. It'll only take a few minutes. Then, when we've got Sally up and had breakfast, we'll go in my car to your flat, wait while you get changed and afterwards drive together to school and I'll take you home tonight. How does that sound?'

'Marvellous. You think of everything, Tim.'

'I try to. The kettle's on. Give Sally a cup of tea.'

A few minutes later, Sally was up. 'Ooh, I feel better now. That must have been food poisoning or something. I'm OK for work though. I'll just watch what I'm doing. I'm sorry to be such a nuisance.'

'Don't be silly. I just don't think you should have seafood again!'

By the time Tim returned, Sally had showered and was looking more like her normal self. She was full of praise for the way he and Claire had looked after her the night before.

They were soon in Tim's car on their way to work, having stopped off first at Claire's flat so she could get changed. Tim parked outside the school. As they stepped from the vehicle another drew up beside them. Claire's heart missed a beat as she saw Adam alighting from his smart Rover.

'Good morning,' he said, his eyes narrowed, looking from one to the other, finally resting on Claire. Without waiting for a reply, he strode off towards the school building.

'He doesn't look very happy today,' Tim remarked. 'I do hope that doesn't mean he's going to give us a bad report. Where was his famous smile?'

'I don't know. He does look a bit grim,' Sally answered, staring after him.

Claire too wondered what was wrong.

None of the teachers came into contact with Adam again that day, but Julia assured them all that he was going to write a good report about the school. Sally soon bounced back to her cheerful, optimistic self.

That evening, when Tim drove Claire home from school, she thanked him once again for the help he had given her with Sally.

'Think nothing of it,' he replied. 'I was glad to be of service. Remember Claire, you can always come to me with any of your problems.'

★ ★ ★

As Claire drove to London on Saturday, she mulled over the events of the past few days. She couldn't forget the way Adam had glared at her when she arrived at school with Tim and Sally. Why did he look so angry? Maybe he'd had a row with his wife. She was also still worrying about whether he would ring her. She hoped he'd forget, but she knew that was unlikely. When Adam said he would do something, he always did it. She decided that if he did ring, the first thing she would tell him was that she was engaged to Martin.

Although she was tired, Claire had set off early that morning. There was little traffic on the road and she arrived at Martin's flat in just over an hour.

He gave her a hug and then led Claire inside where he proceeded to give her a long, lingering hug until she pulled away, saying, 'You're crushing me, Martin.'

'I'm sorry,' he murmured, 'But I'm so pleased to see you.'

Why isn't my heart racing, Claire was thinking? Martin's my fiancé, but I'm not feeling anything. Yet when Adam walked into the room the other day, my heart felt as if it were going to burst. What's the matter with me?

'You're very quiet, Claire. You're not annoyed with me about just now, are you?'

'No. I was thinking what a lucky woman I am.' She threw her arms around Martin, trying to make up for her disloyal feelings.

'That's better,' he said, clasping her hand in his as they sat down on the sofa. 'I was beginning to wonder if you regretted agreeing to marry me.'

'Why should I do that?' Claire asked.

'I don't know, but I've never been able to understand the way a woman thinks.'

'That sounds interesting,' Claire teased. 'Who can't you understand?'

'It's not important.'

'It is, Martin, if you're hiding something from me. I told you about my past. We're going to get married. We should be honest with each other.' You hypocrite! Claire scolded herself. You didn't tell Martin that your former fiancé was the chief inspector and that he's going to get in touch with you.

'Let's not spoil everything by talking about the past,' Martin was saying. 'I don't want to quarrel with you. We're going out to buy your ring this morning. This is a very special day.'

He's keeping something from me and I don't know what it is, Claire was thinking.

Later that morning they went shopping. Claire wanted a sapphire ring. There were many reasonably priced ones to choose from. She would have been happy with any of them, but Martin particularly liked one which had a large sapphire in the centre surrounded by little diamonds. 'Try it on,' he urged.

'I can't. It's much too expensive,' Claire protested.

'I said, try it on. I can afford it. You know I had a good bonus for Christmas.' He picked the ring up and placed it on Claire's finger.

To her surprise, it fitted perfectly. 'It's beautiful,' she breathed.

'Like the person trying it on,' Martin murmured and Claire blushed. 'You see, it's just right. We'll take this one,' he said turning to the shop assistant.

'Certainly, sir. Do you want me to wrap it up?'

'No, thank you. My fiancée will wear it now.'

Claire thought, he's taking over, speaking for me. Is that what my life is going to be like from now onwards? She replied. 'Thank you Martin. It's lovely. I never dreamed that I would own such an expensive piece of jewellery.'

'You deserve it. Besides, my future wife should have something extra special.'

'What can I buy you?' Claire asked.

'Some gold cuff links would be nice.'

Martin chose ones that she could afford. 'Are you sure you want those?' she asked. 'What about these?' She pointed to some more expensive ones.

'No. I like the others best.'

They spent a pleasant day, finishing up at the Barbican for a concert. The final work was Beethoven's Ninth Symphony. 'That's my favourite piece,' Martin remarked. 'The orchestra was superb. I think the London Symphony

Orchestra is one of the best around.'

'I agree,' Claire replied. 'The choir was good too.'

Later when they were back at Martin's flat sipping coffee, she said, 'I've been thinking, I'd love to sing in a choir again. I used to when I was at college.'

'Perhaps, after we're married.'

'I don't want to wait that long. I'll have to see if I can join the Greenhill Singers.'

'But it's not worth it. You won't be in Greenhill much longer.'

'I'm not leaving yet. I've only been there a term.'

'I was hoping we could get married soon.'

'We've only just got engaged, Martin. I want to wait a while. There's no rush.'

'There is. I'm fed up with you leaving me each night. I want you to stay with me, but I can see the only way you'll ever do that is when you marry me. What about an Easter wedding? Then you'll have been two terms at Greenhill.

I could sort it out at the Registry Office next week.'

'The Registry Office!' Claire sounded outraged. 'I'm not going there. I want a church wedding.'

'That's out of the question. I . . . I don't attend church and neither do you.'

'Actually I do go when I can, and I've always wanted to get married in church.'

'I suppose you want a long white dress . . . and a big cake too . . . all that nonsense.'

'It isn't nonsense.' Claire thought, this isn't going to work. We've only just got engaged and we're rowing already. We've both got such different outlooks on life. I hadn't realised that before. Because we have similar tastes in our leisure activities, I believed that we were compatible, but we're not.

'Claire, we're two mature people, we . . . '

'Mature!' She said. 'You're completely taking over and dictating everything.'

'I was just trying to say, we don't

need all those fripperies. The important thing is that we're together. Nothing else matters, Claire.'

'But it does. Don't speak for me. Those fripperies as you call them, are important to me.' She flounced off the sofa and walked to the window. She looked out at the panoramic view over London where the lights seemed to be winking mockingly at her. 'It's time I went home,' she said.

'We can't part like this.' Martin came over to Claire and put his arms around her. 'I'm sorry if I've upset you. I didn't mean to. I didn't realise how you felt.'

'I think there's a lot of things you don't know, Martin.'

'What's that supposed to mean?'

'Nothing.' Claire pulled away from him. 'Forget I said it.'

'I can't do that.'

'You'll have to.' Her voice was waspish. 'I'm tired. I want to go home. I'll get my coat.'

'Can't we make it up?' Martin pleaded.

'All right.' She gave him a quick kiss. 'Will I see you next Saturday?'

'Of course.' Claire looked at his dejected face and felt sorry that they'd had their first row on the day he'd bought her the beautiful engagement ring. 'Thank you for the ring. I don't deserve it.'

'You do. And thank you for the cuff links. I will think about what you said. I'll see you to your car.'

Martin put his arm around Claire and escorted her to the car park where he tried to give her a kiss. She found it hard to respond. She wanted to get away from him so she could think.

'You're still angry with me,' he murmured.

He's right, she thought, but she replied, 'I'm just tired. I'll come at the usual time on Saturday.'

'Good. If it's a nice day we could walk along the Embankment and then have a meal out. That will give us plenty of time to talk. We'll both have calmed down by then. How does that sound?'

'Fine.'

Martin hugged her close and kissed her one more time before saying, 'Drive carefully, Claire.'

She drove off with mixed feelings. She regretted upsetting him and felt mean for doing so, but she was also annoyed. Would they ever be able to sort out their differences? Was he right? They were two mature adults. Did she really need all the trappings of a white wedding in church? Was it so important to her? This thought went round and round in her head until finally she decided it was. If she'd married Adam, it would have been in church.

He'd once said, 'I can't wait to see you walk down the aisle in a long white dress. You'll make the most beautiful bride ever.'

Claire blushed at the memory. Did he say that to his wife? Was she beautiful? Why do I keep torturing myself thinking about Adam? If I hadn't seen him again, I would probably have been quite happy with Martin. Adam's ruined everything. He made it worse by saying that he would ring me. I feel so unsettled. That's why I keep wondering if I should be marrying Martin.

When I hear from Adam I'll tell him straightaway that I'm engaged and say that I don't want him to contact me again. It's not fair to his wife either. Then I hope to get him out of my life for good and I can devote myself to making Martin happy. I wonder why he is so set against a church wedding. Perhaps he'll change his mind when he realises how strongly I feel about it.

★ ★ ★

On Monday morning Claire arrived at school at the same time as Sally. 'Did you have a good weekend?' her friend enquired?

'Yes, thanks. You look a lot better than the last time I saw you,' Claire replied. 'Did you do anything interesting?'

'I just relaxed after the inspection.

Did you see Martin?'

'Yes.'

'Isn't it about time you and Martin got engaged?' she laughed.

Why did she have to say that? I guess I'll have to tell her now. 'Actually we are engaged. Martin bought the ring on Saturday.'

'Oh, congratulations,' Sally beamed as she hugged Claire. 'That's wonderful. I hope you'll be very happy. When's the wedding?'

'We haven't decided yet.'

'Let me see your ring.'

'I'm not wearing it for school. It would get ruined.'

'I suppose so. I hadn't thought of that. All the paint and . . . sand . . . and . . . water.'

'Yes. Teaching's a messy job.'

Other members of staff had arrived at school. Sally called to them, 'Listen, everyone. I've got some good news. Claire got engaged at the weekend.'

They clamoured around wanting to know the details. Claire was quite embarrassed by the attention she was receiving. As soon as it was possible she excused herself, saying she had to prepare for the day's lessons.

At home time that afternoon Tim came into Claire's room and said, 'I've just heard the news. 'Congratulations. I'm surprised though. You didn't give any inkling that you were about to get engaged. It was all a bit sudden, wasn't it?'

'Not really,' Claire answered sharply.

'You don't seem very excited about it,' Tim remarked.

'I'm not the excitable type,' Claire replied thinking, but I used to be.

'If I'd just got engaged, I'd be over the moon.'

'Well, we're all different, Tim.'

'Are you sure you should have got engaged? You didn't just drift into it, did you?' he asked, looking at her intently.

'No, of course not,' she snapped. He's got some cheek, Claire thought. 'What's it got to do with you, anyway?'

'I'm sorry. Maybe I shouldn't have said that, but I was only concerned for your welfare. You know how I feel about you.'

'Tim! That's enough. Find yourself someone else . . . someone . . . who'll be good to you.'

'I wish I could, but it's not that easy. They don't compare favourably with you.'

'Tim!' Claire was feeling embarrassed.

'All right, I'll say no more, but if you ever need someone to talk to, or a shoulder to cry on, I'll be there.'

'That won't be necessary,' she replied.

After Tim had left the classroom, Claire thought, what a muddle I'm in. I seem to be piggy in the middle. Tim's hankering after me. I'm engaged to Martin but still dreaming about Adam, who's married to someone else. Will I ever sort out my life?

During the week, Martin rang and apologised for upsetting Claire. 'I think you were right,' he said. 'Let's just enjoy being engaged for a while. There is no need to rush anything. After all, we're going to spend the rest of our lives together. I'll just have to learn to be patient.'

Claire was glad Martin was taking that attitude, but thought the way he mentioned 'spending their lives together', made it sound like a life sentence. She wanted to appease him however, so she answered, 'In the summer we'll have been together for a year. That might be a good time to plan for the future. Meanwhile, let's enjoy ourselves. Why don't you visit me again one Saturday or Sunday in Greenhill? You haven't been there for ages.'

'Maybe, when the spring comes.'

'That would be lovely. It will be very pretty there when all the bulbs are blooming and the leaves start to appear on the trees again. Greenhill is a very attractive town.'

'Do you work for the Tourist Board?' Martin joked.

'It is a nice place,' Claire insisted, but

she had to smile. 'If you visited me more often you'd know that.'

'I agree, it is a very pleasant town, but it is rather quiet. Don't you think so? You must miss London.'

'Not really. I like the peace and quiet.'

'That might create a problem when we sort out our future. I could never live there. I like the noise and bustle of London. Besides the bank's in London. I don't want to live too far from it. My flat's so comfortable. Could you consider living there, Claire?'

She thought it was a good thing Martin couldn't see her face. His flat was nice enough, modern and luxurious, but when she got married she wanted a house and a garden. There were so many problems they'd have to overcome. She answered,' We said we weren't going to plan our future yet.'

'Yes. You're right. We'll discuss this another time.'

When the conversation ended, Claire

thought, I can see I'm going to be the one who has to make all the sacrifices. Martin wants everything his own way. Can I cope with that?

I don't want a complicated life with constant arguments. Claire sighed, it doesn't sound inviting though. Even Tim thought I didn't seem very thrilled about my engagement. I should be excited, but the trouble is, I'm not.

★ ★ ★

The next few weeks passed pleasantly. The atmosphere at school was much more relaxed. Martin made no further reference to their future plans and the two young people continued meeting at weekends enjoying the time they spent together.

One Saturday after half term, Martin visited Claire. Spring was in the air in Greenhill. Everywhere was green. Buds were bursting into bloom. He seemed very impressed with the town and Claire was beginning to hope that he might change his mind and be willing to live in Greenhill after their marriage, as there was a good commuter train service to London. She also hoped that he might be persuaded to get married in church.

Most of the time Claire managed to put Adam out of her mind, determined that if he rang, she would say she didn't want to hear from him any more. She began to think about her future with Martin and was resolved that she would do everything in her power to make their marriage a success.

The school had received a favourable inspection report and everyone was delighted. Their action plan had been written, explaining what they intended to do to maintain their high standards. They were awaiting a visit from one of the inspectors to discuss the plan with the Head.

At lunch time one day, Claire had been working in her room as usual. Just before afternoon school began, she came out to collect some books.

Ahead of her in the corridor, she saw a figure walking away. Immediately she recognised it as Adam. She wanted to turn round and go back, but she needed those books so she had to carry on. She crept slowly along, keeping her distance, feeling her heart beating faster and praying that he wouldn't see her.

Her prayer was not answered. Adam suddenly stopped, turned round almost as if he knew she was there and walked towards her. 'Good afternoon, Miss Robinson,' he greeted.

Claire mumbled a reply wanting him to go away, but at the same time couldn't take her eyes off him.

He looked round, leaned towards her and whispered, 'I haven't forgotten what I said that day. I've got your telephone number. I will ring you soon.'

She was wondering what to reply when she saw Sally walking towards them. Adam too sensed that someone was coming, so he straightened up and called, 'Goodbye Miss, er, Robinson.'

Then he hurried on, smiling at Sally as he passed.

'What did he want? 'She asked, catching up with Claire.

'Nothing.'

'Well, he must have said something. I saw his head bent towards you.'

'All he said was, 'Goodbye', and he'd enjoyed visiting the school.' Claire hoped this would satisfy Sally.

'He didn't say that to me. I don't suppose we'll ever see him again, worse luck.'

The bell rang for afternoon school so they quickly finished their conversation.

The following weekend Claire and Martin went to stay with his parents. She travelled to London on Friday evening, intending to leave on Sunday. She was greeted warmly by his mother. 'Sit down and make yourselves comfortable, dinner won't be too long,' she told them.

His father gave them a drink and then excused himself saying he had to help his wife. Claire felt completely relaxed and was telling Martin about her week at school, when his mother walked in and asked, 'What plans have you two made for the wedding?'

Claire was pleased that Martin replied, 'We haven't made any yet. There's no hurry.'

'Isn't there?' his mother asked. 'I thought you had to book the wedding well in advance. You know how popular the Registry Office is.'

'Oh, but we might have a church wedding,' Claire answered, 'That is if I can persuade Martin.'

'You haven't told her, have you, Martin?'

'Told me what?' Claire asked.

'I knew this would happen,' his mother snapped. 'I warned you, Martin. You should have explained.'

Claire looked from one to the other, feeling worried, noting that her fiancé had gone quite pale. 'Will someone please tell me what's going on,' she insisted.

Martin spoke quietly. 'I'm sorry Claire, but I've been married before.'

The Heartbreaking Truth

'You've what?' Claire shrieked, unable to take in what she'd just heard.

'I've been married before,' Martin repeated.

'Why didn't you tell me? I guessed you were hiding something but I didn't think of that.'

'I'll go and get dinner ready,' Mrs James said tactfully, moving towards the kitchen.

'Don't get any for me,' Claire called. 'I'm leaving.' She marched over to the door.

'Oh, you can't do that dear. You've only just arrived. Stay and talk to Martin. I know he should have told you, but please listen to him while he explains everything.' She glared at her son. 'If only you'd heeded my warning, all this upset could have been avoided. You should have let Claire know weeks ago, instead of allowing her to find out in this way. I'll leave you two alone. Please say you'll stay, Claire.'

'All right.' She didn't want to offend Martin's mother. Claire sat down and Mrs James walked away.

When they were on their own she turned to Martin and snapped. 'Well, are you going to tell me about it?'

'I'm sorry. I know I should have told you, but I don't like thinking about it.' He put his head in his hands.

'That's no excuse. It's important we're honest with each other. When I told you about my previous engagement, I asked if you had anything to confess, and you said you hadn't. That wasn't the truth. How can we hope to have a happy marriage if you're lying to me before we're even married?'

Martin looked up. 'It's the only lie I've ever told you and it won't happen again.'

'I . . . I'll never be able to trust you.' Claire's voice faltered. 'Why . . . why didn't you tell me?'

'I was ashamed and embarrassed.'

'But you'd asked me to become your wife. How could you hope to keep something like that from me? As you chickened out of telling me before, surely when you found out I wanted a church wedding you should have said something then? You must have realised that it might be impossible. Not all vicars will agree to marry someone who is . . . divorced. I take it you are divorced?'

'Yes, Claire.'

'You were . . . dishonest. I don't understand you, Martin.'

'I'm sorry. What else can I say?' He tried to take hold of her hands but she pulled away.

'I'm sorry too. It's not going to work. There's no trust between us. I think we'd better call the whole thing off.'

'Don't say that,' he pleaded. 'Maybe we can find a vicar or a minister who will agree to marry us. It doesn't have to be Church of England does it? Non conformists are often willing to marry divorcees. I'll do that for you if you want it so much. We'll get over this.'

'You might, but I won't.'

'Let me tell you what happened. Will you listen, please Claire? Try to understand. This is not easy.'

'All right.'

Martin took hold of Claire's hand. This time she didn't pull away. 'I was very young, too young to get married I suppose.'

'And your wife?'

'Jo was a year younger. We met at school. We started going out together in the sixth form and got married as soon as I left university. My mother warned me it wouldn't last and so did my older brother, Peter. In fact he knew she couldn't be trusted, but I wouldn't listen.'

'Oh, I'm sorry Martin.'

'I was young and foolish,' he continued. 'I thought I knew better than everybody else. I was furious with Peter for saying anything against Jo. I thought he was jealous of us and was trying to cause trouble.'

'All the more reason why you should have been honest with me.'

'I know that now. Please forgive me, Claire. I acted stupidly. I do regret it.'

'What happened to your, your wife, Jo?'

'Two years after we were married, she left me for someone else.'

'Oh, how awful!' Claire felt torn between sympathy for him and anger that he hadn't told her the truth sooner.

'I had no idea she was having an affair. It was such a shock. It took me ages to get over it. I was lucky to have so much support from my family. Eventually Jo and I divorced. It's taken me all these years to recover sufficiently to think of marrying again . . . and now . . . I . . . I've ruined everything. Until I met you I imagined I would remain single for the rest of my life. Please forgive me for what I've done, Claire. Is it so terrible that I've been married before?'

'No. I'm not annoyed about that, but

I'm furious that you didn't trust me enough to tell me.'

'It's not that I didn't trust you. It's just that I felt ashamed my marriage didn't work out and that I was ditched by Jo for another man. My pride was badly dented.'

So was mine, Claire was thinking. That was what caused me and Adam to split up.

'I would have told you in the end,' Martin continued. 'I try not to think about those awful years. It still hurts. Can you understand that?'

'Yes, but when you're going to marry someone, you shouldn't keep anything from them.' Claire thought, isn't that what Tim said to me? Am I going to tell Martin about Adam and the real reason we separated? No. That's different. I wasn't married to Adam. We were only engaged.

'Do you think you could forgive me,' Martin was saying.

'I don't know. I'll have to think about it.'

There was a tentative knock on the door. 'Can I come in? Have you sorted things out yet?' Mrs James asked.

'Not really, but do come in. We can talk another time,' Claire replied.

'So you're not going to rush off? Dinner's ready.'

'I'll stay tonight, but I do need to think about everything.'

'Good. You sleep on it, dear. It won't seem so bad in the morning. Come and have your dinner. Martin's dad's starving. Can't wait any longer, he says. Come into the dining room.'

They were unable to continue their conversation that evening. Claire tried to act normally in front of Martin's parents. It wasn't their fault he'd acted so badly she reasoned. Later when he escorted her upstairs and tried to kiss her, she pulled away.

Claire pushed open the bedroom door, hurried inside and locked it behind her. She threw herself down on the bed and sobbed into the pillow. She could hear Martin tapping on the door.

'Go away,' she called.

He kept repeating, 'I'm so sorry, Claire.' Finally when he got no response from her, he gave up and went downstairs.

Why am I so upset, she asked herself? Is it so bad that Martin has been married before? No, it's because he didn't tell me. That's what I'm bothered about, and the fact that I'm not very good at choosing the right man. Adam could have been the right man, but I didn't give him a chance. I just believed the worst and acted like a silly schoolgirl and ran away, and I've regretted it ever since. Am I going to do the same thing with Martin now?

Gradually Claire calmed down. Perhaps I am making too much fuss she thought. Now we've got this out in the open, maybe our relationship will improve. I won't break up with Martin. I'll wait and see how things go. I don't want to act hastily again and then wish I hadn't.

The next morning Claire informed

Martin of her decision and he was very relieved. 'You won't regret it,' he told her.

'I hope you're right,' she replied.

For the rest of the weekend he tried very hard to make it up to her, but Claire was finding it difficult to forgive. I shouldn't feel like this, she kept telling herself. I lost Adam because I was too proud to listen to him. I can't let my stupid pride ruin my life. By the time Claire left Martin to return to Greenhill, she'd resolved to give her engagement another chance. Martin's marriage was in the past.

★ ★ ★

Claire returned to Greenhill and life went on as normal for the next few days. One evening she was busy preparing worksheets for her class when the telephone rang. Picking up the receiver with one hand and continuing to write with the other, she absent-mindedly answered, nearly dropping it when she recognised the voice at the other end.

'Claire, it's Adam. How are you?'

'What do you want?' she squeaked.

'That doesn't sound very friendly.'

'It's not supposed to be. You're an inspector and I'm just a lowly teacher. They're not usually friendly with each other.'

'But you were my fiancée. We were going to get married until you broke it off. Surely we can talk about it now?'

'It was all so long ago,' Claire murmured. 'What's the point?'

'I want to try and understand what happened. I still remember the pain of it all, as if it were yesterday. Can't we meet and talk about it?'

'I don't think so.'

'Why not?'

'You're married for one thing and . . . '

Claire was going to say she was engaged, but before she could finish Adam interrupted, 'Who told you that?'

'Does it matter?'

'No, I suppose not.'

'Actually it was Emma. She found out from Lorraine.'

'So you still thought about me?'

'Well, as you just said, you were my fiancé. But Adam I don't think we should meet. What good can come from it?'

'A lot, I hope.'

'It's too late now.'

'It's never too late, Claire.'

'After you broke off the engagement when you returned to Cyprus I waited for a long time . . . hoping you'd get in touch and explain why you'd left me, but . . . but you ignored my letters. I thought it was hopeless.'

'Well, I couldn't forget what you'd done.'

'What did I do? You never told me.'

'You must know, Adam, but anyway it's too late to go into that now.'

'I really don't know.'

'There's no point in discussing this. You got married, Adam. What happened all those years ago, doesn't matter any more.'

'But it does.'

'No, Adam. It's not fair to your, your wife.' Claire forced the words out.

'I have no wife.' Adam's voice went so quiet she could hardly hear him.

'But . . . but Emma told me . . . '

'I did have a wife and a child but they . . . they died,' he almost whispered.

'Oh, I, I'm so sorry, Adam. I didn't know.' Her voice was full of compassion.

'How could you?'

'Do you want to talk about it?'

'Not now,' he hesitated, 'but I do want to meet you again to find out what went wrong and why you left me.'

Claire felt terrible. She had been so wrapped up in herself and her troubles that she hadn't stopped to consider Adam might have problems of his own. His were much worse than hers. Now she knew why his eyes looked so sad. 'All right, I will meet you,' she agreed, ignoring the little voice in her head which said, you aren't being fair to Martin.

'Good. Perhaps I'll get some answers at last. Which day suits you?' Adam asked briskly.'

'Sunday afternoon or evening would be fine for me, but should you see me? Supposing someone saw us together?'

'The inspection's long over. Besides, who's going to worry about what you and I are doing? Unless of course, there's something you're not telling me about?' Adam replied. 'Like your relationship with Timothy Harding for example?'

'There isn't one. We're just friends,' she answered.

'You two looked pretty friendly that day when I met you getting out of his car. Do you often travel to school with him?'

'That's all we are. Friends and nothing more, and no, I don't often travel to school with him. There was a good reason for it that day, but I won't go into it now. Anyway, why am I telling you this? It's no concern of yours who my friends are.' Claire was thinking about Adam's querying her non-existent relationship with Tim, but he has no idea that she was engaged to Martin.

'Point taken,' he replied. 'I'm sorry, I shouldn't have said that. Sunday's fine for me too. If you let me know your address, I'll pick you up and we could have a meal out or a drink, whichever you'd prefer.'

'A drink will do, thank you.'

'Do you actually live in Greenhill, Claire?'

'Yes.'

'What made you move there?'

'I fell in love with the place the first time I saw it.'

'You remember me taking you there?'

'How could I ever forget?' Claire murmured. Then she continued, 'I was teaching in inner London and in need of a change. Then one day I saw the advertisement for a job at Greenhill Infants School. I applied and fortunately was successful. Where do you live?'

'Ten miles away in Springwood.'

'I've never been there.'

'It's a pleasant enough place, but I prefer Greenhill.'

'Why did you move to Springwood then?'

'My wife's parents lived there. She wanted to be near them.'

'So you didn't achieve your ambition then?' Claire mused.

'What ambition?'

'To live in Greenhill.'

'I'm surprised you remember that. Maybe I will one day.'

They arranged a time to meet and Claire hung up feeling weak and shaky. She had found it much easier to talk to Adam than she'd expected. In spite of the fact that he was now an Ofsted inspector and many years had passed by, she'd been able to speak to him on an equal footing.

What have I let myself in for, she wondered? Adam will be furious when he finds out about Martin. He'll want to know why I didn't say I was engaged. I should have mentioned Martin as soon as he suggested us meeting.

For the next few days Claire wrestled with her conscience. The thought that Adam was free was going round and round in her head. But you're not free, she argued. You promised to marry Martin. You can't let him down. He's been hurt before. He trusts you. But when you got engaged, you didn't know Adam was widowed. You believed he was still married. If you'd known, would you still have agreed to marry Martin?

When she visited Martin the next time, which was the day before she was due to have a drink with Adam, she didn't tell him about it and she didn't break off her engagement either. Claire felt guilty and confused.

'Aren't you ever going to forgive me?' Martin asked, thinking that was why she was acting in such a cool way towards him.

'I'm trying,' she replied.

'I'm sorry if I'm rushing you, but I want things to get back to how they used to be.'

'You should have thought of that before you kept secrets from me,' Claire snapped.

'It was only one secret.'

'Maybe, but a jolly big one.'

'Oh Claire, please don't keep on about it. I've apologised. What more can I do?'

'Nothing, I'll get over it eventually. You'll just have to be patient.'

At home that night Claire reproved herself. If you hadn't been in contact with Adam again, you would have forgiven Martin by now.

She spent the next day preparing for school, but her mind wasn't on it. All she could think of was that she was going to see Adam in the evening.

Claire agonised about which clothes to wear, finally deciding on a new navy trouser suit, with matching suede shoes and a pale blue silk top, which she decided was neither too smart nor too casual. You're only going out for a drink, she told herself, but Adam's an inspector now, he probably dresses more formally. I don't want to look out of place with him.

At eight o'clock Adam arrived dressed in a light grey suit and a black polo necked sweater. Claire caught her breath as she opened the door of her flat and saw him smiling down at her, his blond hair flopping over his forehead in the way that she remembered.

She felt dizzy as she let him in, thinking he shouldn't have this effect on me. Martin doesn't. I've got to finish this before I do something to hurt Martin. He doesn't deserve to be treated badly. Then why aren't you wearing your engagement ring? Did you really forget to put it on?

'I . . . I'm nearly ready,' Claire stammered. 'I . . . I've just got to get my bag.'

'You look charming,' Adam stared intently at her as she blushed. He glanced around her lounge and remarked, 'You have a lovely home. I've always admired these flats.'

Martin has never said that, Claire thought. She replied, 'I think so. I'm very fortunate. It's small but comfortable. Not too far from the shops.' She was glad the conversation had become less personal.

'You have a good collection of CDs.' Adam was gazing at the overflowing shelves.

'I'm afraid I can't resist buying them.'

'You always liked music. We did at least have that in common.'

'We had lots in common, Adam.' Then changing the subject, said, 'We can go now.'

He led Claire to his large, grey Rover car and settled her in beside him. 'I thought we'd drive to an old country inn a few miles outside of Greenhill. It's quite an appealing place for a Sunday evening drink. A log fire, comfortable armchairs and pleasant music. How does that sound?'

'Lovely,' Claire murmured as if in a dream. Was she really sitting in Adam's car, going out with him for a drink? She had never expected this to happen again. Then she remembered Martin and felt overcome with guilt.

Soon they were comfortably seated in the inn, enjoying their drinks when Adam said, 'Now are you going to tell me why you finished with me?'

'At the time I really believed . . . you knew why. Anyway I was much too young to get married. I wasn't ready to settle down. I . . . I wanted to see the world.' That's what she'd kept repeating. She had felt too humiliated to tell him what she thought she'd seen and heard at the time. Months later, she'd realised that she'd probably got it all wrong, but by then it was too late to remedy the situation.

'I know that's what you told me,' Adam answered, 'but I don't believe it. You also kept implying that I'd done something wrong, but you wouldn't say what.'

'It doesn't matter now.'

'But it does. One minute, you couldn't wait to marry me, the next you couldn't bear me near you. What happened, Claire? Was it another man? Although I gather you're not married. You're still Miss Robinson.'

I should have worn my engagement ring. It would have been an easy way, of letting Adam know that I'm not free, Claire was thinking. 'No there was no-one else for me, but I ... I thought ... ' Her voice trailed away. She couldn't say it. She'd feel too embarrassed.

'What did you think?'

'It's not important.'

'Please tell me, Claire. I've waited all these years to find out.'

'Let's just say I changed my mind. That is a woman's prerogative,' she answered quickly.

'I'm not satisfied. If we're going to start seeing each other, again we've got to be truthful and ... '

He wants to see me again, Claire

thought, but I'm engaged to Martin. How can I tell him that now? Oh, what a mess I'm in!

'So, do you want to see me again?' he repeated.

'I, er, don't know,' she stuttered. 'We've changed. We're different people. You're an inspector now and I'm just an ordinary teacher.'

'You've never been ordinary to me, Claire.'

She blushed and continued, 'Whatever made you become an inspector? I can't understand that.'

'It wasn't in my plans either, but after you left me, I threw myself into my career, eventually becoming a Head teacher. Then someone suggested I train for Ofsted. I debated long and hard with myself and was finally persuaded when it was pointed out, that someone has to do the job, so it might just as well be me.'

'You used to hate inspections as much as I did.'

'Yes, but I resolved to be gentle. I

thought I'd do a good job and show everyone what an inspector should be like. I hope I've succeeded.' Adam hesitated, 'but I'm not sure.'

'Well, the staff at my school thought you were very fair.' Claire put her hand over her mouth and gasped, 'Oh, I suppose I shouldn't have said that.'

'No, it's all right. Thank you for telling me. I'm glad you did.' Adam took hold of Claire's hand and stared into her eyes. 'I still can't believe I've found you again. I thought I'd lost you for good.'

She looked away, not wanting to see those piercing green eyes, which seemed to be probing into her soul. She felt like a traitor. Whatever she did, someone would be hurt. She knew she should tell him about her engagement, but couldn't bring herself to do it, and if Martin found out that she was seeing Adam he'd be horrified.

'What really happened, Claire? Please tell me. Nothing makes sense.'

'It doesn't matter now. It was so long

ago. Anyway, you soon got over it. You made a new life for yourself,' Claire answered defensively.

'I never got over it.'

'But you married someone else.' She pulled her hand away.

'Yes, well, what did you expect? That I'd be lonely for the rest of my life, pining over you? Was that what you thought would happen? You knew I wanted a wife and a family. Was I supposed to wait in case you changed your mind?'

'No, of course not.'

'I waited a long time, hoping you'd reply to my letters, but you didn't.'

'When I returned from Cyprus I did try to get in touch, but you'd moved and I couldn't find out your address.'

'I even asked Bella about you,' Adam continued.

'You asked Bella?'

'Yes. I thought she might be able to shed some light on the situation. I guessed you'd keep in contact with her. You two had been friends for years. I . . . I . . . '

'What did she say? Claire interrupted.

'That you were having a wonderful time in Cyprus, that you'd met all new friends. I wished I hadn't asked.'

'It wasn't true, Adam,' she couldn't let him go on. 'None of it was. I hated it at first. I was so miserable.'

'And you didn't meet anyone special?'

'No. How could I? I still kept thinking about you.'

'So why did you tell Bella that?'

'Because I couldn't admit to anyone that I'd made a terrible mistake.'

'I don't understand any of this. Why did you leave me?'

'I can't talk about it now, Adam. It's in the past . . . over.' Claire felt close to tears. She didn't want to remember all the heartbreak she'd experienced so long ago.

'I don't know what to think,' Adam continued. 'I believed you didn't love me any more. I thought my case was hopeless.'

'So you married someone else.'

'You told me to. Remember? Our last telephone conversation.'

Claire couldn't forget. In a fit of jealous rage she'd shouted, 'Marry someone else. Go to, to . . . your . . . ' She hadn't finished the sentence. She couldn't bring herself to say the words.

'I remember,' Claire whispered, tears springing into her eyes. 'I shouldn't have said that. I didn't mean it.'

'How was I to know that? If you'd given me any hope, I would have waited for you to come back.' Adam took hold of her hand again.

Claire held onto it not knowing what to reply. She couldn't look at him. If she saw those green eyes filled with passion, she was frightened she would forget her obligations to Martin. She didn't trust herself and her feelings for Adam.

'Oh Claire, can we start again?' He was saying. 'It's not too late, is it?'

'I don't know. I'm so confused.

149

'Why? Because I married someone else?

'Perhaps.'

'I thought everything was over between us. I had to make a new life for myself. I was only doing what you told me to do.'

'I know,' Claire murmured. She was doing that too, making a new life for herself with Martin, but now she'd met Adam again, would anything ever be the same between her and Martin? 'Can you tell me about your marriage or is it too hard for you to talk about it?' Claire asked quietly.

'I'll try, but it's a very sad story.' Adam sighed. 'Do you really want to hear it?'

'Yes. Please tell me if you can.' She squeezed his hand.

Adam took a deep breath and began. 'My wife's name was Beth. I met her at a friend's party. She was also tiny and blonde. Rather like you. She was working in London as a secretary, but she became ill and went to stay with her parents in Springwood so they could look after her.'

'So was that why you moved there?'

'Yes. We thought it best for Beth to be near them. As soon as she recovered, we got married and I started my job as an inspector. Springwood and Greenhill come under the same geographical region so I have to be prepared to cover both areas.'

'Oh, I see.'

'Beth was the same age as me,' Adam continued. 'We got on well right from the start. Soon we were spending all our free time together and it just seemed the natural thing for us to get married. I was in my thirties by then. I'd spent years building up my career after you left me. I wanted to settle down.'

'Did you love her?' Claire whispered.

'Yes, of course, but not in the way I loved you. I was more mature by then. I'd vowed never to let myself get hurt again, but in the end I . . . I had to . . . suffer even greater pain.' Adam's voice faltered.

Claire took hold of his hands. 'What happened?'

His shoulders slumped and he stared down at the table as he continued, 'About three months after we were married Beth became pregnant. She went to the hospital for a check-up and . . . ' Adam gulped, 'They told her that she had a serious heart condition and being pregnant could make it worse.'

'How awful!' Claire was full of concern for Adam.

'We'd no idea she was so ill.'

'What did you do?'

'Beth and I both wanted a baby so much. We were convinced that everything would be all right.'

Adam's eyes filled with tears and Claire wiped one from her face as he continued in a whisper. 'Beth had to go into hospital straight away so she could be monitored night and day. She . . . she never came home again.' His voice broke. 'At thirty-five weeks she went into labour, but it was too much for her. They were worried that the baby had suffered a lack of oxygen.'

Claire couldn't stop the flow of tears now as she held Adam's hands. 'You don't have to say any more. I can see it's too painful,' she told him.

'No. I want to go on. I haven't been able to talk about it till now.' He choked back a sob. 'The baby, a girl, Bethany lived for only two days.'

Claire felt tears running down her face. 'I can't begin to imagine how you coped with the shock of it all. It makes my problems look so small.'

'When something like that happens you feel numb. Nothing seems real any more. I just threw myself into my work and tried not to think of anything else. I was jolted back into reality when I walked into your classroom and saw you.'

'I'm sorry. Perhaps it would have been better if you hadn't seen me.'

'No. I wouldn't say that. For years I've wanted to find out why you finished with me, but it seems you're still reluctant to tell me. Am I so difficult to talk to, Claire?'

This is your chance, Claire told herself. Tell him about Martin. Don't hurt him again. 'Adam, I, I have . . . '

'Beth wouldn't have wanted me to be miserable for ever,' Adam interrupted Claire seeming not to have heard her answer. 'I've got to start living again.'

'Thank you for telling me about Beth.' Claire squeezed Adam's hand.

'It's your turn. I want to hear what you've been doing for the last five years. You've never married?'

'No.' Tell him, a little voice in her head kept urging, but she couldn't do it. Not now after the sad tale he'd just told her. 'My life hasn't been as eventful as yours. I enjoyed teaching in Cyprus for a time, small classes, well-behaved children.'

'I've been honest with you, but you won't tell me what really happened.' Adam shook his head. 'Women! I don't seem to understand them at all. I didn't want Beth to risk her life.'

'But she would have resented you.'

'Perhaps, but at least she'd be alive. I feel so guilty. By wanting a family, I caused her death.'

'You can't believe that, Adam. She wanted a child.' How strange all this is Claire was thinking. I'm trying to comfort Adam, forgetting my problems, which seem so trivial in comparison. 'When did all this happen?'

'Just over a year ago.'

'So when you came to my school it was only a few months afterwards?'

'Yes. I immersed myself in work and tried not to think of anything else.'

'You haven't had time to grieve properly.'

'I suppose not. You sound like a counsellor now.'

'Did you see one?'

'No. I didn't want to talk about it. You're the first person I've told. People know I'm a widower, but they're not aware of the circumstances. I was too distraught to say much, and they were too tactful to ask. I feel better though for getting it off my chest. Thank you, Claire, for being such a good listener.' He brushed his lips against her cheek and sat back watching her reaction.

She hadn't moved away from him, although her conscience told her she should. 'I'm glad I've helped,' Claire murmured, as her heart thumped madly. She was amazed that he couldn't hear it.

'I still can't believe that you were at Greenhill Infants School when I came to inspect it. What a coincidence! For years I'd visualised meeting you again, but the way it happened was totally different from anything I could ever have imagined.'

'I know what you mean. I feel the same way too.'

'Perhaps it was meant to be.'

'Do you think so, Adam?'

'I'm so confused. I'm not sure. All I know is that if Beth had lived I would have devoted myself to her and our . . . our child and I would have put you out of my mind. But she, she's gone and now I've met you once more, I don't want to let you go.'

'Oh, Adam.'

'Then,' his voice sharpened, 'I remember what you did and I don't want to go through all that pain and suffering again.'

'I'm sorry, Adam.'

'Are you really?'

'More than you'll ever realise.' He's confused, Claire thought. So am I. He wants us to get back together. How can I? I'm engaged to Martin. What am I going to do?

Suddenly, Adam looked at his watch. 'It's nearly eleven o'clock. We'd better go.'

'Yes. I've got to get up for school in the morning.'

'And I'm starting a new inspection tomorrow. Thank you for everything, Claire. Next time I won't talk so much. It will be your turn.'

'Is there going to be a next time?'

'I hope so. Will you see me again, Claire?'

'Yes,' she blurted out, ignoring her

conscience which was telling her to refuse. 'Next Sunday if that's all right with you, I'll cook lunch.'

'That's an offer I can't refuse. I remember your cooking,' he smiled.

You're playing with fire, Claire was thinking. What would Adam say if he knew you were engaged? And what would Martin say if he knew about Adam? She didn't want to answer those questions. She tried to put them from her mind and concentrate on the present.

They were both quiet on the journey back to Claire's flat, deep in thought about the events of the evening. Adam escorted her to the door. He looked down, gazed into her eyes and said, 'Goodnight Claire, thank you for listening. I'll see you next Sunday.' Then he gently kissed her cheek and hurried away.

A Time For Truth

Claire couldn't sleep that night. Thoughts of Adam, Beth and Martin whirled round and round in her head. She should have told Adam about Martin and felt guilty because she hadn't. However, she knew that if she had, Adam would not have suggested seeing her again. He was a man of honour and wouldn't have wanted to come between an engaged couple.

In the end, Claire gave up trying to sleep. She went into the kitchen, made herself a milky drink and got out a pen and some notepaper. She decided to write down her thoughts and feelings, hoping that once they were on paper, she would be able to come to some conclusion and know what her course of action should be.

She wrote *Martin* on one side and *Adam* on the other. Then she sat staring at the paper. After a few minutes it came to her quite clearly. There was only one thing she could do. She didn't need to write anything down. She had to break off her engagement.

Claire knew Martin would be terribly upset and felt awful about that, but he was not right for her. She should have realised this before. Her love for Martin was not strong enough. Seeing Adam again had confirmed that. The problem was how could she tell Martin this?

There'd be a dreadful scene when she did. I'll break off my engagement on Saturday Claire decided. Then by the time I see Adam on Sunday it will be all over. Eventually I'll tell him about Martin, but not yet.

Claire resolved to discuss with Adam why she'd left all those years ago and ask him to give her an explanation for what she thought she'd seen. She'd realised too late that she'd probably been mistaken. She'd apologise for hurting him and ask if he would give her a second chance. She'd do her best to prove that she still loved him. With this plan in mind, Claire went back to bed and managed to sleep for a few hours.

* * *

At school the next day Claire met Tim in the car park.

'You look very pale. Are you feeling all right?' he asked anxiously.

'Yes, I'm quite well thank you, maybe a bit tired, that's all.'

'Ah, what have you been up to at the weekend?' Tim smiled and Claire blushed.

'Nothing,' she mumbled.

'How's your fiancé? Surely you saw him?'

'Yes, and he's all right.'

'Have you set a date yet?'

'No. There's plenty of time.' Claire wondered what Tim would think if he knew that she was going to break off her engagement in a few days and get back with Adam Black, their former Ofsted inspector. That would really shock him.

'If I was engaged I'd want to get things sorted out straight away, especially if . . . if you were my fiancée.'

Claire didn't like the way this conversation was going so she quickly changed the subject. 'What was your weekend like, Tim?'

'Rather boring. I stayed at home.'

'Why don't you join a club or something? You might meet some nice people.'

'Maybe, but there's only one person . . . '

Tim didn't get a chance to finish the sentence as Sally rushed up saying, 'Hello you two, I'm a bit late this morning. Couldn't get out of bed.'

Claire was relieved to see her. 'Did you do anything exciting?' she asked as they walked into school and arrived outside Sally's classroom.

'Yes. I've joined a rambling group. We went out for the day yesterday. We walked from Greenhill to Clayfield, about nine miles. That's why I'm exhausted. I'm not used to it.'

'That sounds like hard work,' Tim remarked.

'Yes, but afterwards we had a meal in a lovely old inn. It was great. Most of the other ramblers are young and I've met lots of new people.'

'It'll be worth getting all those blisters on your feet then?' Tim mocked, regaining his usual jovial manner.

Sally laughed. 'Do you enjoy walking, Tim?'

'Yes, but I don't do it very often. It's not much fun on your own.'

'Why don't you come along one Sunday and see if you like it. There's a lot of girls.'

'That sounds like an offer you can't refuse,' Claire smiled. 'I've been telling Tim he needs to join something,' she said to Sally.

'How about it then?' she asked.

'All right, I'll give it a try. You two girls have persuaded me. I'll go next Sunday, if you'll come with me Sally?'

'I will,' she replied. 'What about you, Claire?'

'No, sorry I can't come.'

'I suppose you'll be seeing Martin.' Sally commented.

'Er, yes,' Claire lied. She had more important things to do like cooking dinner for Adam and trying to put things right between them.

'That's a date, Tim. I'll hold you to it.' Sally looked at her watch. 'I can't stand here talking any longer. I've got to get my classroom ready for the onslaught.' She hurried away and Tim followed.

As Claire walked into her room she was feeling pleased that Sally seemed to be taking Tim under her wing. If she keeps him occupied, maybe he'll find himself a girlfriend and then he won't have to pester me.

He's a likeable chap, he deserves someone nice. It's no good him pining after me, especially now I intend getting back with Adam.

Claire liked that thought. She felt amazed that he wanted it to happen. She guessed he must have forgiven her for leaving him. She would have to try to explain why she'd done it.

At the time she believed she had good reason for it, but later she realised she'd misjudged Adam, especially when she'd heard from some of her friends, but by then it was too late to do anything about it.

* * *

When Saturday came, Claire travelled to Martin's flat with dread in her heart. How could she tell him that she wanted to break off their engagement? She didn't want to hurt him, but it had to be done.

As soon as she arrived he pulled her into his arms holding her until she broke away saying, 'That's enough, Martin. You're making me breathless.'

'Sorry, but I'm pleased to see you. I've missed you so much. I'll be glad when we're married and can be together all the time. This waiting's driving me mad. Can we set a date? Please, Claire?'

'No, Martin. I . . . er, I think . . . '

'Shush. Don't spoil everything.' He put his finger on her lips. 'I won't say any more about it today, but remember what I've said. I know you're still mad with me for not telling you about my marriage, but I'll make it up to you. I promise you there are no more secrets.' Martin kissed her lightly on the cheek. 'I've got some tickets for the theatre, a matinee. Then we could have a meal. How does that sound?'

'Fine,' Claire murmured. She'd lost her chance of telling him. When would she be able to do it?

She'd have to wait until after the show now, but that wouldn't be easy.

They went to the theatre. Martin enjoyed the performance, clapping enthusiastically at the end, but Claire couldn't concentrate. She was busy rehearsing in her mind what she was going to say to Martin.

Afterwards he suggested, 'Let's walk along the Embankment. We had that huge ice cream in the interval. I'm not hungry yet. Dinner can wait.' He took hold of her hand. 'Let's make the most of this lovely weather.'

Claire breathed deeply. This was her opportunity. She had to take it. 'Martin . . . '

'Yes?'

'There's something I have to say.'

'What is it? You look very serious.'

'I am serious. I know you won't like this but . . . '

'No, Claire. Please don't spoil this evening.' His voice was gentle and pleading. He stopped walking and turned to face her.

She had to go on even though she was overcome with guilt. 'I'm so sorry Martin, I . . . I . . . '

'What are you trying to say?'

'I, can't . . . '

'You're going to tell me you don't want to marry me,' Martin interrupted harshly. 'Is that what this is about?'

'Yes,' she whispered.

'I've known there was something wrong all day. Your face gave you away.

But we can get over this, Claire. I've told you that.'

'No Martin. It won't work.'

'Why?'

'We're not right for each other.'

'I could make you happy. I know I could.'

He wasn't listening to her. 'That's the problem. We wouldn't be happy.'

'You're wrong, Claire.'

'No. It's because we . . . '

'All right. I know it's my fault,' he blustered impatiently, 'But you've got to forgive me.'

'Listen, Martin, it's not because you didn't tell me you'd been married before. Yes I was annoyed about that, but it made me realise we weren't suited. We want different things out of life.'

'I think we're well suited.'

'I'm sorry Martin, but I mean this. I want to break off our engagement before I hurt you any more.'

'You seem to make a habit of doing that. Getting engaged and then changing your mind.' His voice was hostile.

'Do you get some kind of pleasure out of it?'

'That's not fair. Of course I don't.' She couldn't blame him for thinking it though. 'It's better to call things off now rather than finding out after the wedding that we've made a terrible mistake.' Claire quickly removed the engagement ring from her finger and handed it to him. 'I'm sorry I should never have agreed to get engaged in the first place. I just sort of drifted into it.' That was what Tim had said, she thought. He was right. 'Please take this.'

Martin snatched the ring and thrust it into his pocket. Then he pulled the cuff links out of his shirt, the engagement present Claire had given him. 'Here, you'd better have these back. I can't believe it. I never thought that you of all people would do this to me. I've been so wrong about you.'

'I'm so sorry,' she murmured.

'That's my lot with women. I'm finished with them,' he exclaimed bitterly.

'You'll meet someone else one day.'

'I won't. I don't think I want to now.'

'Look, Martin. Can we go back to your flat? I think it's best I leave.'

'If that's what you want. We'll give dinner a miss. I couldn't eat a thing if I tried.'

They walked along in silence, both keeping as far apart as possible on the narrow pavement. Claire was glad that Martin hadn't made a scene. She glanced up at his face. He looked stunned, as if he were in shock. She felt dreadful knowing it was all her fault.

When they got back to Martin's flat Claire collected her things. 'I'm sorry I've hurt you,' she said.

He didn't say a word. He just stared after her as she hurried to her car, a look of abject misery on his face.

On the journey home Claire knew she had done the right thing in breaking off her engagement. She wished that she hadn't let their relationship go so far. She'd been swept along by Martin. He'd pressurised her and she shouldn't have given in to him.

Even if Adam hadn't come back on the scene, Claire was convinced that marriage to Martin would not have worked out. One day he would realise he was better off without her.

★ ★ ★

The next day Claire arose early. She hadn't slept well and was glad to get up. She had to make preparations for the week ahead at school, and then she could concentrate on making lunch for Adam.

She remembered that pork had always been a favourite of his, so she cooked some cutlets in wine and roasted a selection of vegetables, and also made a fruit cake as he liked that.

Claire was a good cook but in the week she didn't have a lot of time so she ate simply, often just enjoying a salad. On Saturdays recently she hadn't cooked as she'd been visiting Martin, so Sunday was the only day she could put her culinary skills into practice.

Claire was feeling excited and nervous at the same time. Butterflies were racing round her stomach, but there was also a delightful feeling of anticipation.

She reflected that she'd never felt like that when she'd been going to meet Martin. She should have realised there was no spark of electricity between them. It was only when she met Adam again that she understood what was missing from her relationship with Martin.

At half-past twelve precisely Adam rang the bell. Claire hurried to the door, her heart thumping. She was wearing a pale blue close fitting dress which suited her slim figure perfectly, the colour matching her sparkling eyes. She smoothed her blonde hair catching a glimpse of her flushed cheeks in the hall mirror. This was going to be a momentous day. She prayed that everything would go well.

Claire opened the door and Adam

stood gazing down at her, an expression on his face which to her was unfathomable. 'You look wonderful,' he breathed.

She thought he looked magnificent too, but declined to say it.

He kissed her lightly on the forehead, followed her into the flat, thrusting a huge box of Belgian chocolates into her hand.

'Thank you, Adam. My favourites. You remembered,' she murmured. 'You'll have to help me eat them though, otherwise I'll put on too much weight.'

'I shouldn't worry about that, you're so slim. What's the delicious smell coming from the kitchen?' Adam sniffed appreciatively.

'Lunch is nearly ready.'

'I can't wait. I didn't have much breakfast this morning. I remembered what a brilliant cook you were.'

Claire smiled. 'I hope you won't be disappointed.' She hadn't eaten much either, but for a different reason, she'd been too excited.

She led him into the lounge and told him to sit down.

'Can I help you?'

'No thank you. I can manage. I won't be long.' She didn't want him in the kitchen. She wouldn't have been able to concentrate on what she was doing.

Soon they were enjoying their starter, broccoli and pepper soup, which Claire had made, using her newly purchased blender. Conversation flowed freely as they ate their lunch and Claire felt pleased that everything had gone so well.

'That was the best meal I've had in ages,' Adam remarked as he finished his last mouthful of fresh fruit salad and ice cream. 'Can I make the coffee while you have a rest?'

'I thought you were good at cooking,' Claire replied.

'I'm not bad, but you're much better.'

'Thanks Adam, but I'll make the drinks. It won't take long.'

'Hurry back. We've a lot to talk about.'

'Have a look at my CDs. Choose something you like.'

When Claire returned with the coffee, she saw Adam sitting on the sofa looking very relaxed. He'd chosen an easy listening disc of light classical music. 'That's a good choice,' she told him as she placed the cups on the table. She seated herself opposite him in one of her comfortable armchairs.

'The Warsaw Concerto's on it . . . my favourite.'

'Yes, I remember.'

Adam sipped his drink thoughtfully. 'I try to play it on the piano myself sometimes, but I don't practise enough. Do you still play? I noticed your electric piano in the corner.'

'Not as much as I should. Can't find the time.'

'It's a lovely day, Claire. Shall we go for a walk after our coffee?'

'That would be nice. We could go to Greenhill Country Park.'

'Yes, it'll be beautiful there now. All the spring bulbs and blossom will be in bloom.'

'They are,' she replied. 'I drove past the other day. Greenhill is such an attractive place.'

'I've always thought so, even when I was a small child, yet I've never managed to live there. You've beaten me to it.' Adam sounded pensive.

'I know how lucky I am. I was just in the right place at the right time. The first time I looked at the job vacancies, I saw the advertisement for Greenhill Infants School, so I knew I had to apply. I couldn't believe it when I heard I'd got the job.'

'Did you have much difficulty finding this flat?'

'No. Again I was lucky. It was all so easy. The rent is cheaper than in London. Everything fell into place. It seemed as if it was meant to be.'

'Perhaps it was,' Adam murmured.

'Do you think so?'

'Yes. Sometimes things happen and

at the time we don't understand why, but later we can see a reason for them.'

'If I hadn't moved to Greenhill, I wouldn't have seen you again. Do you think this was meant to be, Adam?'

'I'm not sure. I hope so.'

'If I hadn't left you, you wouldn't have married Beth.'

'I suppose not.'

'Wasn't that meant to be?'

'I don't know.'

'I think it was.' Seeing the brooding expression which had crept into Adam's eyes, Claire changed the subject. 'Would you like another coffee?'

'Please.'

When she returned from the kitchen with his drink, Adam seemed more composed. He was studying the books on the shelf.

'What's your house like?' Claire asked.

'It's pleasant enough. Three bedrooms, large lounge, long garden, but too much for me now I'm on my own. It's a family house. I've thought about moving, but haven't been able to bring myself to do it. I feel as if I have been through a long dark tunnel, and I'm only just beginning to see the light at the end.'

'That's not surprising. You've had such a terrible experience.'

'I seem to have gone from one bad thing to another in the last five years,' he sighed.

Claire saw the anguished look on his face and wished she hadn't asked about his home. 'It's partly my fault,' she added.

'I won't deny that,' he answered bitterly.

'I'm sorry.'

'I keep wondering why I'm here,' Adam continued as if he hadn't heard her. 'After what you did, I shouldn't have any more to do with you. I must be a glutton for punishment.'

'I feel so guilty.'

'If you would explain to me why you left me, I might be able to understand it all.'

Ignoring that remark Claire went on, 'It was better that you didn't marry me five years ago.'

'Why? What do you mean?'

'Because of Beth.' Claire was surprised that all her bad feelings about Adam's wife had disappeared. Now she could only feel great sadness for her. Previously, she'd been consumed with jealousy, even though she knew it was irrational. After all, it was partly her own fault that he had married Beth.

'I don't think I understand your logic,' Adam was saying. 'I never did. Women's thoughts are on a different wavelength to men's.'

'Well, I'm sure you made Beth happy for the short time you were together.'

'I hope so,' he murmured.

'Don't you see? It was meant to be. If you'd married me, Beth wouldn't have had that happiness.'

'No, but she might still be alive.'

'You'll never know that.'

'I suppose not, but what a tragedy!' Adam leaned across towards Claire and took one of her hands in his. 'I'm sorry we keep getting back to my problems. You should tell me to be quiet.'

'I'm pleased you feel you can talk to me.'

'I don't know what to make of you.'

'Why?'

'You seem like the old Claire in some ways, but I'm sure you're keeping something from me and I don't know what it is.'

'That's enough serious talk.' Claire pulled her hand away. 'How was your last inspection?'

'You keep evading giving me an answer. I won't probe any more today, but I won't be satisfied until I know the truth. My inspection,' he continued, 'went very well. It was in Springwood, quite near where I live actually.

'All the schools in this area are very pleasant. They don't have the problems that we used to face in London. I'm sorry I gave you a hard time at your inspection. I was so astounded at seeing you again, that I reacted badly.'

'I guessed that. It was a shock for me too. I didn't know how to carry on normally.'

'You did very well.'

'Should you be saying that?'

'Why not? Your inspection's over. The report's been written. I'm not saying anything I shouldn't.'

For the next half an hour they chatted about work. Claire was amazed at how easily they were talking together. It was almost as if they had gone back five years to the time before everything went wrong.

'How are your parents?' Adam asked. 'I used to be very fond of them.'

'They're both dead.'

'Oh, I'm so sorry. What happened? They weren't very old, were they?'

'No. They were in their sixties. Although Elizabeth is ten years older than me, they'd married very young. They, they were killed,' Claire's voice faltered, 'as a result of a car accident.'

'How awful!' Adam took hold of her hands.

'It was such a shock. They were driving home one evening about two years ago after visiting friends. It was a dark road. Another vehicle smashed headlong into them.

It was found out later the driver had been . . . been drinking.' Claire stifled a sob. 'My father died immediately but my mother survived a few days, dying in hospital without regaining consciousness.'

'Poor Claire. What a waste of lives. You must have been devastated.' Adam put his arm around her.

'I was. One day you have two parents and then suddenly you're an orphan. It was unbelievable. Do you remember my sister, Elizabeth? She invited me to stay with her in Scotland whenever I liked.'

'Yes, I remember her.'

'I often go there during school holidays. She phones me regularly. She's the only living relative I have left.'

'I haven't many either, just a few cousins. I'm an orphan too.'

'Your parents have died? Oh, I'm

sorry. I didn't know. You've had so many tragedies in your life, Adam. I'm so sorry.' She was full of sympathy for him but also felt pangs of remorse, knowing that her behaviour had only added to his suffering.

Adam stood up. 'I think we've talked enough for the moment. If you've finished your coffee Claire shall we go for a walk?'

'Yes. That's a good idea. I'll fetch my jacket.'

She was putting it on, when the doorbell rang.

'You weren't expecting anyone, were you?' Adam asked.

'No, of course not. I've no idea who it can be.' What bad timing, she thought. I'll have to get rid of whoever it is quickly.

'Aren't you going to answer it?'

'All right. You wait there. Sit down a minute. I won't be long. It's probably someone selling something. They keep coming round here touting things. Give me a minute.'

Claire reluctantly walked to the door, pulled it open and gasped as Martin threw his arms around her, kissing her passionately.

'Does He Feel
The Same Way?'

Claire fought to get away from Martin's grasp but he was too strong for her. 'Stop it,' she muttered, not wanting to make too much noise, hoping Adam wouldn't hear them.

'I've come to make a peace offering,' Martin said when he finally released her. He bent down, picked up a huge bouquet of red roses and thrust them into Claire's hands. 'These are for you. I'm really sorry for what I did. I was wrong in not telling you about Jo.' He attempted to put his arms around her again, but she quickly dodged away. 'Claire, what's the matter?'

'No Martin, I can't take them.' She handed the flowers back. 'It, it's . . . '

'Don't look like that, so reproving,' he interrupted, taking the roses as he stared down at her. 'I've said I'm sorry. What more can I do? Please forgive me. We can start again. Let's wipe the slate clean. We can't leave things as they are. I've been awake half the night planning what to say to you.' He moved closer to Claire. 'Can I come in? We don't want the neighbours to hear our business.' Martin started to push against the door, but she stepped in his way.

'There's no point. It's over between us.'

'No, Claire, let me come in, please. We need to discuss this.'

'There's nothing to discuss.' She stood firm.

However, Martin was equally determined. 'Just give me half an hour. You owe me that at least. I've travelled all the way from London to see you. If you would just give me a chance I'm sure I could persuade you to change your mind.' He was still clutching the flowers.

'We're finished. Can't you understand that?' Claire raised her voice, thinking how can I get rid of him? Adam must be wondering what's going on. Why did Martin have to come at this precise moment? Everything had been going so well with Adam. 'Please go, Martin,' she begged.

'I've brought your ring back. I want you to have it.' He sounded desperate.

'I don't want it, we're . . . '

Before she could say any more, the lounge door burst open and Adam was standing beside her. 'Is everything all right? Are you having trouble? I heard you raising your voice.' He turned to Martin. 'Who's this?'

'I was about to ask who you were,' Martin snarled. 'Claire, what's going on?'

She stepped aside and sighed, 'You'd better come in.'

'That's what I wanted in the first place, but I didn't know then you had company. Is this one of your work colleagues? Are you going to introduce me?'

Claire took a deep breath. How was

she going to get out of this tricky situation? In all the months she'd been going out with Martin, he'd never turned up unexpectedly. It wasn't the sort of thing he did. He lived an orderly, well planned life. It hadn't occurred to her that he might do this.

Claire also couldn't help thinking that now it was too late, Martin seemed to have woken up and was displaying a greater degree of passion than expected.

As he entered the lounge, Claire saw his frown deepen as he looked round the room and noticed the remnants from lunch, two dirty plates and other dishes still on the table. He pushed them aside, throwing the flowers down beside them. Then he placed the ring back into his pocket.

'This is Adam Black,' she murmured wearily. 'Adam, this is Martin James.'

'Pleased to meet you,' they said simultaneously with icy politeness, as they eyed each other up and down. Both men were very tall, but one so dark, the other so fair.

'I've heard that name somewhere before, 'Martin muttered, a puzzled expression on his face. 'Do you work with Claire?'

'Not any more,' Adam answered briefly, staring at Claire's pale face.

She was looking from one to the other, feeling as if she were having a nightmare.

'I remember now,' Martin remarked half to himself. 'Claire told me her inspector was called Adam, but he was a real tyrant. It must be a popular name. How did you come to meet her?'

'We were friends a long time ago,' Adam replied without taking his eyes off Claire. In fact, we were . . . '

'So you're another teacher?' Martin interrupted.

'Not exactly. I, I'm . . . the tyrant.'

Claire slumped down into an armchair, not knowing what to do or say.

Martin's mouth fell open in shock as Adam asked, 'And who are you? How do you know Claire? She wasn't expecting anyone. We were about to go out for a walk when you arrived.'

'You! The . . . the inspector?' Martin gasped. 'I don't understand. What are you doing here?'

'I could ask the same question,' Adam retorted, getting the upper hand as he turned to Claire and demanded, 'Who is this?'

Before she could reply, Martin who had recovered his dignity and was bristling with rage, spat, 'I'm her fiancé.'

'You're what?' Adam shouted.

'Claire and I are engaged, but what that's got to do with you, I can't imagine.'

'We were engaged, Martin, but not any more,' she said quietly, hardly daring to look at Adam, as she waited for his reaction.

'He was your fiancé? You didn't tell me about this. Why not, Claire? When was this?' Adam snapped.

'It's over, that's why,' she whispered,

knowing that any hope of a reconciliation with Adam had been completely dashed.

'Oh, so you're fed up with him and have broken it off, just like you did with me. Is that it?'

Martin gazed at each of them in turn, his anger replaced by bewilderment. He could see the look of despair etched on Claire's ashen face and the haughty demeanour which Adam had now adopted.

'What are you talking about?' Martin asked at last.

'For your information, Claire used to be my fiancée too,' Adam answered his eyes like steel. 'She seems to make a habit of leading a man on, getting engaged and then ditching them.'

Claire could contain her feelings no longer. 'That's not true.' She choked back a sob.

Adam ignored her and marched to the door stating, 'I'm leaving.'

She ran over to him, grabbed his arm and pleaded, 'Please don't go, Adam. I can explain everything.'

'I bet you can, a little schemer like you!' He disentangled himself, opened the front door and walked out, slamming it shut as he called, 'Goodbye, Claire.'

She couldn't stop herself from crying. The tears fell down her face. She'd never heard Adam speak in that bitter, sarcastic way before.

Martin had followed Claire to the door and had observed Adam's departure. 'I can't believe it.' His face was full of scorn. 'I trusted you but while we were going out together, you were carrying on with, with him. That's why you would only see me on a Saturday. I suppose you spent every Sunday with that man or have you got somebody else in tow too?' he exploded, not giving Claire a chance to defend herself. 'And if I hadn't turned up unexpectedly, I'd never have known.'

'No, Martin. That's not true,' she sobbed. 'I haven't been seeing Adam or anyone else behind your back. It wasn't like that.' Tears were pouring down her cheeks.

'You, you of all people! I wouldn't have believed you could be so deceitful.'

'Come into the lounge, Martin, and I'll try to explain.'

She led the way. He stomped along behind. Claire perched on a chair and he sat opposite hunched up with his head in his hands.

'I'm sorry, Martin. I didn't mean to hurt you.'

'But you have. Why did you do it, Claire?' He looked up, fixing his eyes on her as she squirmed and burst into fresh sobbing. 'Do you like having power over men? Does it make you feel good?'

'No,' she whimpered. 'I know you won't believe me, but I didn't want this to happen.'

'Then why did you have to go as far as getting engaged? That's what I'd like to know.'

'You're not being fair, Martin.' Claire quickly sprang to her defence. 'You begged me to get engaged. I tried to tell you I wasn't ready but you wouldn't listen,' she flared.

'Well, I didn't know then what a schemer you were. Adam Black was right about that. He's walked out on you and I'm going to do the same. At least I know now it's not worth losing any more sleep over you. You're on your own. You've got what you deserve, but I suppose there'll soon be some other poor man tagging along.' Martin's face was contorted with rage.

Claire hadn't realised before that he was capable of such a depth of emotion. She felt overwhelmed by guilt at the way she had treated him, but at the same time, she knew he was not entirely blameless. After all, he was the one who kept insisting they got engaged, even though she'd wanted to wait.

She was also feeling devastated by Adam's departure, knowing that was her fault too. She'd made a complete mess of everything and had no idea how to resolve it. She wiped her eyes and fresh tears streamed down her cheeks.

Martin stood up and strode to the door. 'It's no good you blubbering,' he said unkindly. 'You've asked for this.'

'You won't let me explain,' Claire murmured. 'I know it's over between us, but I really didn't want it to happen this way.'

'What is there to explain? You want to tell me about all your past affairs? Is that it? So you can gloat over me?' Martin was beside himself with rage. He attempted to open the front door, but Claire held onto his arm.

'Please listen. I know I've been stupid, but I owe you an explanation. Come and sit down.'

Martin hesitated and she let go of his arm. 'How many fiancés have you had then?'

'Only two, you and Adam,' she whispered.

'But you told me that you were engaged to someone five years ago.'

'I was . . . to Adam.'

'I don't understand.'

'If you'll come and sit down, I'll try to explain it all. Please, Martin.'

'All right.' He slumped into an armchair.

Claire sat uncomfortably on the edge of her seat not daring to meet his gaze. 'I met Adam when I first started teaching. You and he are the only two men I've ever been interested in. There's been no-one else.'

'So what happened?'

'We got engaged after he became a deputy head at another school, but it didn't work out,' she added hastily. That explanation would do for Martin but not for Adam she thought.

'Poor devil! I suppose he rushed you into an engagement too when you weren't ready.'

'Something like that,' Claire murmured.

'But I still don't understand. If you finished with him all those years ago, what was he doing here today?'

'I saw him again at my school inspection and after it was all over, he asked me to meet him.'

'You mean you hadn't kept in touch with him?'

'No. When our engagement ended, I went to Cyprus to teach. I didn't see him again until he walked into my classroom.'

'Why didn't you tell me he was your inspector?'

'Because you weren't very interested in the inspection and I thought he was married.'

'Is he?'

'He's a widower.'

'So you've been going out with him while you've been engaged to me?' Martin said bitterly. 'And I didn't suspect a thing. You should have been an actress, Claire.'

'No,' she protested. 'That's not true.'

'How many others were there?'

'I told you, none.'

'So it was just a coincidence, seeing Adam again?'

'Yes. It was such a shock.'

'It must have been. But why was he here today? You've been meeting him behind my back?'

'No. This was only the second time,' Claire murmured. 'Once I saw Adam again I realised I wasn't being fair. I knew I should never have agreed to marry you. That's why I broke it off yesterday. I'm so sorry, Martin.'

'You still have feelings for him after all this time?' he asked incredulously.

'Yes,' she whispered.

'What about Adam? Does he feel the same way?'

'I don't know.'

'How long has he been a widower?'

'About a year, I think. There was such a lot we needed to talk about. I told you, apart from the inspection, this was only the second time I've seen him.'

'Now, you won't be able to discuss any of it. He's gone too.'

Claire nodded.

'Oh dear, we are a pair!' Martin took

hold of her hands. 'We've both made a mess of our lives.'

'I have,' she replied, 'but you haven't. What happened was all my fault.'

'No. I'm to blame too,' Martin said gallantly. 'I shouldn't have rushed you into getting engaged.' He stood up. 'I think I'd better go home. Thank you for being honest with me, Claire. I'll have some explaining to do to my parents. They were staggered when I told them what happened yesterday. It was my mother who urged me to come today.'

'I'm sorry I put you through all this.'

'So am I. It's been such a shock. I was furious at first, but now I don't know what I feel.'

'Thank you for being so understanding.'

'I'm not really. I'm traumatised. There's no point in ranting and raving, it won't change anything. The truth is, you prefer Adam to me.' Martin walked to the door and opened it. 'Goodbye, Claire.' He walked away without looking back, his shoulders hunched in misery, making him seem somewhat smaller.

Claire watched from her window until he had disappeared from view. All his self confidence seems to have oozed away she thought. I shouldn't have done this to him especially after he told me about his broken marriage.

She felt consumed by guilt and full of concern for Martin, but underpinning this was the knowledge that her bungling had driven Adam away too. Martin was right, she told herself. You're all alone. You've not only lost Adam but Martin as well.

She looked at the flowers he had given her and wondered what to do with them. They were still on the table where he had thrown them, red roses, her favourites.

She remembered the way Adam had frowned when he saw them. I should put them in a vase she thought, but felt more inclined to dump them in the bin. Lacking energy, in the end she did nothing.

Claire sat down in a daze. How could one's life change so quickly? Just a short time ago she'd been ecstatically happy. Everything had been going very well with Adam and she'd begun to believe that they might get back together. Now it was too late. She'd lost her chance. Adam had gone. His parting words to Martin were still ringing in her ears.

'She seems to make a habit of leading a man on, getting engaged, and then ditching them.'

Is this what Adam thinks? Perhaps it does seem like that to him, but it's not the truth. When she'd left Adam she'd believed she had a valid reason for doing so. It was much later when it was too late to do anything about it that she'd discovered her mistake.

For a long time Claire sat inert, unable to do anything, too tired even to cry. Several hours later she dragged herself to bed, where she tossed and turned restlessly all night.

The next morning the flowers were

wilting on the table so she threw them in the bin, feeling this was a symbolic action signifying the end of her relationship with Martin and any other man. She couldn't have Adam. She'd never stop loving him so there was no point in getting involved again.

She'd make a new life for herself. She didn't need a man. Plenty of women managed on their own, so would she.

★ ★ ★

When Claire arrived at school, Sally was already there. 'I can see you've had a busy weekend,' she remarked. 'You look exhausted.'

'Nothing,' Claire muttered hurrying into her classroom. I'll have to tell her about Martin some time, she thought, otherwise she'll keep on about him, but not today. I can't face up to it yet.

She managed to keep out of Sally's way and avoided Tim for a few days.

There was only one week left till the Easter holiday. Claire was glad of that.

She felt in need of a break although in some ways it had been a good thing that she'd been able to immerse herself in teaching. This had stopped her dwelling too much on her personal unhappiness. Once in the classroom all other thoughts had flown from her head. That was the way it had to be.

One evening the telephone rang. It was Martin.

'I didn't expect to hear from you,' Claire told him.

'I guessed you'd be surprised, but I wanted to know if you were all right.'

'Why shouldn't I be?' she snapped, immediately regretting her sharp attitude. Her misery was of her own doing. He wasn't to blame.

Before she could apologise he said, 'Please don't be like that, Claire. I'm feeling so guilty about what happened. I shouldn't have turned up uninvited at your flat on Sunday. I spoilt everything for you. I know it's Adam you want, not me. Why did you break off your engagement to him? What went wrong?'

'I can't go into that now.'

'Have you heard from him again?'

'No. I don't expect to.'

'It's all my fault,' Martin groaned.

'Not really.'

'But it is,' he insisted.

'I was the one who was wrong. I should have told you about Adam and that I'd seen him again. I was furious with you for not telling me about Jo and yet I acted in the same way. There's no excuse. I behaved very badly.'

'Don't be too hard on yourself, Claire. I'm as much to blame as you. Can't you explain all this to Adam?'

'No. He doesn't want to have any more to do with me.'

'So, we're both on our own?'

'Yes.'

'We, we could, just be friends.'

'That wouldn't work. It's best if we make a clean break.'

'Why?'

'Because you will want more than I can ever give you.'

'I suppose you're right.'

'I am. Thank you for ringing me. I'm sorry I treated you this way. I shouldn't have got engaged. I gave you false hope. I didn't mean to hurt you, Martin.'

'I realise that now. It was my bad luck that Adam had to come along again. You can't help your emotions any more than I can.'

'You're being too nice to me.' Claire brushed a tear from her eye.

'Well, you are the girl I wanted to marry. I love you. I can't just turn off my feelings.'

'Oh, Martin,' she choked. 'I'm so sorry.'

'Please don't cry. I'll get over it. I'd better hang up now before I get too emotional. Goodbye, Claire. I hope things will improve for you.'

She collapsed onto the sofa sobbing uncontrollably, clutching the cushion trying to find some comfort. She felt worse because he'd been so kind and understanding. If Martin had ranted and raged it would have been what she deserved.

Her conscience was pricking with remorse. She'd treated him unfairly. She hadn't understood him at all. Now that it was over between them, he'd told her he loved her. She hadn't expected that, believing his feelings for her were rather shallow. Claire asked herself why is it that you only appreciate something when it's too late? It was no comfort for her to know that she'd done exactly the same thing with Adam.

* * *

On the Friday before the Easter holiday, Claire was tidying her classroom when Tim came in. Since her broken engagement she'd spoken very little to him or Sally. She didn't want to discuss what had happened with anybody yet.

'How's everything?' Tim enquired. 'I haven't seen much of you recently.'

'I'm fine,' she lied. 'How are you? Have you been out rambling with Sally's group?'

'Yes. Last Sunday. It was great, lots of fresh air and good company.'

'I'm glad you enjoyed yourself.'

'You ought to come one day, if your fiancé will let you, or you could bring him along too.'

'Was Sally there?' Claire asked steering the conversation away from more personal matters.

'Yes. She's fallen for one of the new members,' Tim laughed. 'And he looked quite taken with her too.'

'What's he like?'

'Grant? He's nice enough, tall, fair and good looking. Now I come to think about it, similar in appearance to Adam Black actually, but a good few years his junior, so he's more suitable for Sally. She certainly seems to change her affections very easily.'

'That's because she's young.'

'Sounds as if you're talking from experience, are you?'

'Well, I can still remember being Sally's age,' Claire smiled.

'You poor old soul!' Tim bowed. 'I

must give Grandma the respect she deserves. I didn't know you were so ancient.'

'I'm not.' She threw an exercise book at him.

He quickly dodged out of the way and said, 'That's the first time I've seen you smile for ages.'

Claire thought he was right, she hadn't felt like smiling recently and she hoped no-one else had noticed. 'You always make me laugh, Tim,' she answered.

'I don't know whether that's supposed to be a compliment or an insult.'

'A compliment of course. You have a witty answer for everything.'

'I try to, but seriously Claire, are you all right? You've looked rather grim the last few days. You haven't had a row with Martin, have you? I'm not prying, I just want to help.'

'Nobody can,' she blurted out, immediately regretting it when she saw Tim's concerned face.

'I knew something was wrong. Will it

help to talk about it?'

'No. Forget I said it. I'm going home now.' Claire picked up her bags and hurried to the door, giving him no chance to reply. 'Goodbye, Tim. See you after the holiday.'

As she got into her car for the homeward journey she was thinking, I've got to get a grip on myself. People are beginning to notice my moods of despair.

★ ★ ★

Claire decided to telephone her sister. She'd been putting off telling her the news about her ill fated engagement, but knew it had to be done.

When Elizabeth heard she sounded quite indignant. 'Another broken engagement! What's the matter with you? Why can't you settle down and get married like everyone else?'

'A broken engagement is better than a disastrous marriage,' Claire retorted.

'But you're getting on for thirty.

You're not a teenager. You should know your own mind by now.'

Claire came off the phone feeling worse. She'd get no sympathy from her sister.

Shortly afterwards Elizabeth had rung back to apologise, suggesting Claire spent a few days in Scotland as there was something she particularly wanted to talk about.

Claire finally agreed after making her sister promise not to nag her about Martin. A few days later she travelled there by train. In spite of her inner turmoil she enjoyed the holiday in Edinburgh. The weather was fine.

The two women spent many pleasant hours walking around the city and countryside. They went shopping in Prince's Street, visited Holyrood Palace and the castle. Elizabeth's husband, Brian, worked long hours and she was glad to have the company of her sister.

Claire noticed that her sister had put on some weight. It suits her she thought. In fact I've never seen her looking so well. Claire also was feeling better. The colour had come back into her cheeks. I'm at a crossroads, she told herself. I must put the past behind me and forge a new life ahead.

Whenever Claire asked Elizabeth what she wanted to discuss, all her sister would say was, 'It can wait.'

So she said no more, feeling pleased that Elizabeth had kept her promise and hadn't questioned her about Martin. Her sister seemed happy, contented and very easy to get on with. Claire decided that she must be mellowing as she was getting older.

Then a few days later the surprise came. The two women were sitting relaxing after breakfast when Elizabeth suddenly announced, 'It's about time I told you my news.'

'At last' Claire exclaimed. 'What is it, Liz? You look quite excited. You've gone bright pink.'

'I am excited. I've been dying to tell you, but it didn't seem appropriate with your broken engagement, but now you look so much better, I can't wait any longer.'

'Go on,' Claire urged. 'What are you trying to tell me?'

'I'm going to have a baby.'

'You're what?'

'I'm expecting. Don't look so shocked. I'm not too old, you know.'

'Of course you're not. That's wonderful news, Liz, but I am surprised. I didn't think you and Brian wanted children.' Claire hesitated, 'I . . . I take it you're pleased?'

'Over the moon. I can't believe my good fortune,' Elizabeth babbled.

'I'm so happy for you.' Claire put her arm around her sister. 'I'm going to be an auntie. That's wonderful.'

'Thank you,' Elizabeth continued. 'We were beginning to think it was never going to happen for us, Claire.'

Claire hugged and kissed her sister. At least one of us has some good news she thought. 'When is the baby due?'

'The end of July. You'll be a good

auntie. I expect you'll be trying to teach the baby to read before it's a month old.'

★ ★ ★

The next few days passed quickly. Claire was annoyed with herself for not noticing her sister's condition. She guessed it was because she had been so wrapped up in herself and her own troubles. She helped Elizabeth get organised for the new arrival, shopping for the baby and selecting items for the nursery.

Claire was thrilled for her sister, but couldn't help feeling a little envious of the happiness Elizabeth and Brian shared. If Martin hadn't turned up that day, maybe Adam and I would be planning our future together she thought, but quickly chided herself for dwelling once again on her problems, instead of focusing on her sister's good fortune.

Elizabeth came to the station to see Claire onto the train for her homeward journey.

213

'I'll come back on the twenty-second of July so I'll be able to look after you for the last few days before the baby's born,' she told Elizabeth.

'I'll probably be as big as a bus by then,' her sister laughed. 'I'll need all the help I can get. Let's hope you have some better news. Perhaps you'll have made it up with Martin.'

'That definitely won't happen. I'm finished with romance for good,' Claire stated vehemently. 'I'll devote my life to looking after my little niece or nephew. That will be much easier.'

To Claire's relief the whistle blew for the train to depart so there was no time for Elizabeth to reply.

'Take care,' she shouted as the doors closed. She stood waving until the train disappeared from view.

★   ★   ★

Claire returned home feeling refreshed, ready for the new school term. She'd received no messages from either

Martin or Adam. She hadn't really expected any but had secretly hoped there might be one. Although Claire knew she'd done the right thing in telling Martin that they couldn't just be friends, she missed him a great deal as he'd played a big part in her life for some months.

She also wished that Adam had given her a chance to explain about Martin, but realised that she'd only got what she deserved. Claire tried to convince herself that in time she would get over all this and her life would improve.

On the first day back at school Claire bumped into Tim in the playground, 'You look better,' he said.

'I am.' She was in the middle of telling him about her stay in Scotland when Sally came along.

'Hello, you two. You'll never guess who I saw in the holiday.'

'Tell us,' Tim urged. 'You look quite excited.

'Well, I went to a dance near Springwood last Saturday . . . '

'With Grant?' Tim interrupted. 'We missed you both at the ramblers' group. We had a good evening. There were a few new people. Sorry Sally, you were saying?'

'Yes, I was with Grant,' she said coyly. 'We didn't think anyone would miss us. Anyway, we went to a dance.'

'Of course we missed you. So who did you see?'

'Adam Black.'

'Oh him,' Tim groaned. 'Surely you're not still interested in him? I thought you'd got Adam out of your system.'

Claire could feel her heart racing as she looked at Sally waiting for an answer. Even now everything was over between them she couldn't hear Adam's name mentioned without getting herself into a state.

'Well he was rather gorgeous and he was at the dance with . . . ' Sally paused.

'Go on, tell us. You do like making a mystery. Who was Adam Black with?' Tim asked.

216

'His wife, and the two of them were so wrapped up in each other that he didn't see me or anyone else I should imagine.'

Being Alone

Claire's heart missed a beat. Adam was with another woman! He didn't waste much time, she thought. Just a short time ago he said he wanted to continue seeing me. Now after that stupid misunderstanding he's found someone else already. Then it occurred to Claire that maybe he was going out with her at the same time. Surely Adam wouldn't do that? He'd suffered so many tragedies in his life that maybe he'd changed.

'Did you speak to Adam?' Tim was enquiring.

Claire tried to concentrate on Sally and Tim's conversation.

'No. I didn't want to intrude,' Sally replied. 'They looked so cosy together. Adam's a brilliant dancer and she's very good too. I had to watch them. She's a lucky woman. I still find it hard to believe that he's an Ofsted inspector. Don't you, Claire?'

'Er, yes,' she mumbled, wanting to scream, 'that wasn't his wife,' but not daring to.

'He couldn't take his eyes off her,' Sally continued.

'I thought you only had eyes for Grant now,' Tim remarked. 'So how come you had time to watch them?'

'We were sitting out that dance to get our breath back so I couldn't help seeing. I told Grant all about Adam and he watched too. He agreed that they looked right together. I'm glad they're getting on well now. Do you remember when we had our inspection, he had such sad eyes? We wondered if he'd had a row with his wife. Well, he doesn't look sad now.'

'It seems to me you spent all the inspection speculating about Adam Black's private life. I don't know how you had time to do that, we had so much paperwork to get through,' Tim answered.

'I like finding out about people,' Sally defended herself.

'Sounds to me more like being nosy. Anyway, I can't waste time with you two girls discussing Adam Black. I've got things to do; the children will be coming in soon.' Tim strode off towards his classroom leaving Sally looking deflated.

'I suppose I should have expected him to pay little attention to my news. I'll have to tell Gina and Lucy later. They'll be surprised,' Sally continued. 'When he was at our school I thought he was interested in you, Claire, but I got that wrong. He's obviously very much in love with his wife.'

Although Claire was feeling shocked by what Sally had told her she had to ask, 'What was Adam's wife like?'

'Attractive . . . petite . . . very young with beautiful long, dark, curly hair, and she was gazing up at Adam as if she couldn't believe her good fortune. He was holding her close giving one of his glorious smiles. Some people have all the luck,' Sally sighed.

Claire was trying hard to keep a rein on her feelings. Her whole world had been turned upside down by Sally's news. She knew now without a doubt that her relationship with Adam was finally over.

He never would ring and apologise. She'd not be able to explain about Martin. Adam had found someone else! Claire didn't want Sally to suspect anything so she forced herself to say, 'But you have Grant.'

'I know and he's lovely, but there's nothing wrong in dreaming is there?'

'No, of course not,' Claire replied, thinking, that's all I can do now.

She found it hard to concentrate on her job that day and the time seemed to drag interminably. The children were still in holiday mode, not wanting to settle down to the restrictions of school life.

When at last Claire reached home she allowed her emotions to take over. She lay on the sofa and gave in to feelings of anger, despair and pain. She shed bitter tears that all her dreams had been shattered, but she was also furious with Adam.

For so long she'd given him the benefit of the doubt, believing she'd been too hasty in calling off her engagement, and that her initial reactions years ago to the incident had been wrong. Now she was beginning to think that maybe she'd been right and that Adam had been deceiving her.

In the midst of her anguish Claire was vaguely aware of the telephone ringing but felt far too distressed to answer it. If it's important they'll ring back again later she told herself.

When she'd been staying in Scotland she'd convinced herself and Elizabeth that she had got over her heartbreak, but now she knew she hadn't. She'd been secretly longing for a reconciliation which would never take place.

After a time, rage took over. She banged her hand down on the coffee table so hard she broke a finger nail.

Was history repeating itself? How could Adam do this to her? Leading her on, letting her think he still cared for her. His feelings couldn't have been very deep if a short time later he had his arms around someone else. Men! She couldn't understand them. She was better off without Adam or any other man.

Eventually Claire calmed down. She trudged to the bathroom to wash her face, comb her hair, repair the broken nail and change out of her crumpled clothes. She was debating with herself what she should eat, feeling that everything would taste like sawdust, yet knowing she needed something. A ring of the doorbell startled her. She felt tempted to ignore it, not wanting anyone to see her ravaged face, but it rang again more persistently, so she decided she'd better answer it.

She opened the door and to her surprise saw Tim standing outside. 'I'm sorry to bother you,' he mumbled sheepishly, 'but I've left my National

223

Curriculum I.T. folder at school and I need it to plan for tomorrow's staff meeting. I wondered if you had ... ' His voice trailed off as he became aware of Claire's pink face and puffy eyes. 'Are you all right?' His voice was full of concern.

'Why shouldn't I be?' she snapped. 'I'm getting my dinner ready, been peeling some onions.'

'Oh, I see. Have you got your folder, Claire? I know I'm a bit of a nuisance, but ... '

'I think it's on the shelf,' she interrupted. 'Come in and I'll have a look.'

Tim followed her into the lounge. She saw him glance through the open kitchen door and guessed he was looking for the onions, but he didn't make any comment.

'Yes, it's here,' she said handing him the folder. 'I don't envy you, having to lead the meeting tomorrow. I hate doing that.' Claire was feeling pleased with her performance. Inside her heart was breaking, yet here she was making polite conversation with Tim as if everything in her life was normal.

'I'll be glad when it's over,' he sighed. 'It's all a waste of time, if you ask me, but it has to be done, I suppose.'

'I agree with you. We spend too much time on all these meetings.'

'I hope you didn't mind me coming round, Claire. You're a real help. I did try ringing earlier but you must have been out shopping or something.'

'No. I didn't mind. I'm pleased I've been of use. Would you like a coffee?'

'I don't want to give you any bother. I know you were getting your dinner ready when I arrived.'

'It will be no trouble,' she assured him. 'I'd love a cup of coffee myself. Dinner can wait.'

'Thanks, Claire. Then I'll join you.'

'Sit down, Tim. It won't take long.' She walked into the kitchen to switch on the kettle.

But Tim didn't sit down. Instead he followed her into the kitchen, his eyes glancing round at the empty work surfaces. He walked up to Claire and stopped, putting his hands on her shoulders, turning her round to face him. 'You weren't peeling onions, were you? You've been crying. I don't want to intrude but it sometimes helps to talk. What's wrong, Claire?'

'It doesn't matter, Tim. You're too observant. I don't want to bore you with my problems.' She pulled away from him and busied herself preparing the drinks.

'You won't bore me. I just want to help.'

'You can't do that?'

'Why? Is it Martin? Has he upset you?'

Claire knew it wasn't going to be easy fooling Tim. He was too perceptive; letting him think that she was in a state over Martin seemed to be the best option. 'Yes. I, I've broken off our engagement.'

'Oh, I am sorry. You must be devastated. No wonder you look so distraught.'

'I am.'

'Poor Claire!' He moved towards her again and took hold of her hand. 'I'd like to help if I can. I hate seeing you so upset. Was it a mutual thing?'

'Not really. I just realised we weren't right for each other.'

'Well, I thought all along you weren't ecstatic enough about it.'

So it was that obvious, Claire thought. Hearing the kettle coming up to the boil, she let go of Tim's hand and started to make the coffee. To her surprise she found herself having to resist the temptation of rushing into Tim's arms.

What's come over me she thought? I'm heartbroken about Adam, yet thinking of falling into Tim's arms! She blushed at the thought. I'm in such a muddle. I don't know what I want. I can't lead Tim on though. I've hurt enough people. 'Coffee's ready.' She tried to sound cheerful as she placed the cups on a tray.

'I'll carry them into the lounge,' Tim replied.

They sat in silence on opposite sides of the room drinking, Claire not wanting to meet Tim's gaze in case he could read her mind. His dark eyes were full of compassion. He'd make someone a lovely husband she reflected, but not her.

'Would talking about it help?' he asked after a few minutes.

'No. I don't think so.'

'I won't pressurise you, but remember I'm always there if you need me, Claire.'

'Thank you Tim but I'll be okay. Don't waste your time worrying about me. I'm no good for you.'

'I'll be the judge of that. I know this is not really the right time but I want you to know that you're always in my thoughts.'

'Tim, please don't say any more.' Her eyes filled with tears. She couldn't handle this now.

He leapt up, rushed over to her, enfolding her into his powerful arms, beseeching, 'Please don't cry. I can't bear to see you unhappy.'

Claire knew she shouldn't, but in her anguished state she relaxed leaning against Tim, feeling safe in his embrace, sobbing as if her heart would break. All the while he held her close, stroking her hair murmuring, 'It'll be all right, Claire.'

Gradually she ceased crying and pulled away from him horrified at what had happened. 'I'm sorry, Tim. I shouldn't have done that.'

He too looked embarrassed. 'It was my fault. I was so upset at seeing you cry. It . . . it won't happen again.'

'No, it mustn't,' Claire reiterated. 'You're too kind to me. I don't want to hurt you.'

'Why would you do that?'

'I seem to make a habit of it.'

'I can't believe that. I suppose you're talking about Martin?'

'Don't mention him again.'

'I think I'll go if you're feeling better.' Tim walked to the door. 'I've got that preparation to do for tomorrow.'

'Yes, of course. Sorry I kept you.'

'You didn't. I stayed because I wanted to and now I'm leaving because it's safer for you if I do.'

'Tim!'

'Goodbye, Claire. Thanks for the coffee.'

He let himself out as she stared after him, her emotions churning. She felt ashamed of herself, allowing Tim to embrace her, although he had acted the perfect gentleman and had only been trying to comfort her. He was not to blame in any way.

She was the one in the wrong because she knew Tim had feelings for her and she shouldn't have encouraged him. Perhaps that was her trouble. She led men on. Adam had said that after the row with him and Martin. Maybe he was right. She didn't mean to do this but somehow it just seemed to happen. She'd have to make sure it didn't occur again, particularly with Tim. It wasn't fair to him.

It would have been so easy to give in.

He'd have been good to her, but she didn't love him and never would. She had nothing to give him or anyone else any more. It was ironic that both Tim and Martin wanted her, but the one man she was interested in, no longer cared about her.

From now on she'd be alone. Plenty of people managed on their own. She could too. She still had her career and her sister and now there was the birth of Elizabeth's baby to look forward to.

★   ★   ★

At lunch time the next day, Claire sat in the corner of the staff room eating her sandwiches when she heard Sally telling Gina and Lucy about seeing Adam at the dance.

'His wife's a lucky woman,' Gina was saying.

'Yes, I've never seen a couple look so in love,' Sally replied dreamily.

'Yet when Adam was here, you kept

remarking on what sad eyes he had,'
Jenny added.

'Well, he did then.'

'I expect he was going through a bad
patch with his wife. It happens
sometimes, you know. They've probably
made it up now,' Lucy said.

'That sounds like it,' Gina agreed.

'Oh no! You're not still discussing
Adam Black are you? The inspection's
long over. Forget him.' Tim had entered
the room and had heard the women's
remarks. 'Let's talk about something
else.'

'You don't understand! Men never
do,' Sally snorted as she and the other
two walked out of the door.

Tim marched straight over to Claire
and whispered,' How are you?'

'Fine thanks, and you?'

'I'm always well. Fit as a fiddle, that's
me.' His brown eyes searched Claire's
face and then he added, 'But I'll be glad
when tonight's over.'

'The staff meeting? You're not really
nervous about that are you?' She was

glad he hadn't talked about anything more personal.

'I'm nervous about a lot of things,' he responded, 'Especially . . . '

Before he could continue Claire interrupted, 'Nonsense. I don't believe it, a big tough man like you?' She smiled, 'I'll have to go, Tim. Got to sort out my classroom.'

'I'll give you your folder back before the meeting,' Tim answered.

'Thanks. See you later.' She hurried away.

That evening Tim escorted Claire to her car. 'About yesterday,' he started, 'I think we need to talk.'

'There's nothing to discuss,' she answered. 'Forget what happened.'

'I can't. You know how I feel about you.'

'Tim, we're friends, good friends and that's all.'

'You seemed more than just a friend yesterday.'

'I'm sorry. I was overwrought. I shouldn't have let it happen.'

'I'm not sorry.'

'But I am.'

'Look, Claire. I know you're upset about Martin and this is probably very bad timing, but maybe eventually . . . ' he hesitated, 'you . . . you could think of me in a different way?'

'Shush, Tim. The others are coming. They'll hear what you're saying. And the answer's no. Please don't mention it again.' Claire quickly got into her car and drove off feeling guilty that her actions had given the wrong impression and this time it was Tim she'd hurt. I'm going to have to keep out of his way she decided. It's difficult us both working in the same school, but I like it here. I don't want to change jobs.

* * *

Claire was careful to avoid Tim as much as possible after that and he seemed to take the hint. There were no more embarrassing episodes. He was becoming quite involved with Sally's rambling group for which she was very grateful. Claire genuinely liked Tim and had been flattered by his attention but didn't want him wasting time on her. She was a hopeless case. Thoughts of Adam still dominated her waking hours and she tried in vain to quell them.

Gradually life settled into a pattern. Claire was glad that her career took up most of her time. Occasionally she would go out with Sally or one of the other teachers from her school, but apart from that she led a rather solitary life.

Claire telephoned Elizabeth regularly to make sure she was keeping well. One day her sister enquired, 'Haven't you and Martin made it up yet?'

'That will never happen,' she answered.

About six weeks after the break up, Martin rang Claire to see how she was. 'Any news of Adam?' he'd asked.

'No. There won't be,' she told him.

'I was hoping that by now you'd be back together. I realise it was my fault that you split up. It's on my conscience.'

'Don't let it be. I wasn't honest with him or you, so I got what I deserved. I'm resigned to it now. Don't worry about me, Martin.'

'But I do. I don't want you to be unhappy.'

'I'm not. My job takes over my life. I've no time for anything else.'

'That's still the same then,' he replied. 'Your career always came before me.'

'I'm sorry, but that's how it is with teaching these days. What are you doing now, Martin?'

'Going out with some chaps from work for a drink occasionally, that's about all. Claire?'

'Yes.'

'I've been thinking. You're on your own in Greenhill and I'm on my own in London. Why don't we get together some time?'

'It wouldn't work.'

'I'm not so sure. We could take it

slowly. I wouldn't rush you into anything. That was my mistake last time.'

'But Martin, you know I haven't got over Adam.'

'You will in time. Think about what I've said, Claire. It makes sense. Promise me you will. You don't have to answer now.'

'All right, but I won't change my mind.'

That night in bed Claire thought about Martin's suggestion. She was tempted to accept his idea. It would ease her loneliness, but she couldn't risk hurting him again. She didn't love Martin. It was still Adam and always would be.

★ ★ ★

It was May. Claire was out one day when she spotted a poster advertising a concert in Greenhill Parish Church. She asked some of the female members of her school staff if they would be interested in going, but none were.

Claire particularly liked the pro-gramme so decided to go on her own.

On the day of the concert she made herself look very smart. It's the first time I've dressed up in weeks, she thought as she put on some make-up and styled her hair.

She donned her new lilac suit with its short skirt which showed off her slim legs and ankles. I must do this more often she told her reflection in the mirror. I've been in a rut. It's time to start living again.

Claire arrived early, sat down in a pew near the front of the church, perused the programme, and admired the architecture of the building.

'What a lovely surprise. I didn't expect to see you here, Claire,' a familiar voice interrupted.

She glanced up at Tim who was looking very dashing in a grey suit. He smiled down at her and asked, 'Are you on your own?'

'Yes.'

'Can I sit with you?'

'Of course. Do you like classical music, Tim?'

'I love it, especially Beethoven.'

'Oh, I should have thought jazz was more in your line.'

'Don't look so astonished, Claire. I like that too, but I prefer classical music. You see, our tastes in music are similar.' Then changing the subject he added, 'It's nice to see you out and about again. I must say you look stunning tonight.'

She blushed but felt pleased that someone appreciated the care she had taken with her appearance. 'You look good yourself,' she said graciously.

'Thank you. I'm glad you're not moping around the house.'

'There's no point in doing that. It won't change anything,' she stated vehemently.

Suddenly a suspicion formed in her mind. Had Tim known she was going to the concert? She'd been careful to only mention it in the staff room when he wasn't present, but maybe somehow or other he had found out.

'I've been really looking forward to this,' Tim was saying.

'Me too,' Claire replied wishing the music would start. A worse thought occurred to her. Had she been set up by her so-called friends? They all knew about her broken engagement and on the whole had been very tactful, but could someone have decided to do a bit of matchmaking and pair her off with Tim?

'This is a lovely church,' he said. 'Look at those beautiful stained glass windows. They're exquisite.'

They continued to make polite conversation until the orchestra started to play. Then Claire became engrossed in the music. She was remembering concerts long ago when she'd been with Adam. They'd sat holding hands, enraptured and lost in their own world. Then she recalled other concerts when she'd been with Martin. He had a different approach, wanting to analyse the music rather than let its emotion wash over him. This had irritated her at the time.

'Let's just enjoy it,' she'd begged. 'I don't want to dissect every bar. That spoils it for me.'

Claire glanced at Tim to see what his reaction was, but to her embarrassment she met his intense gaze. She quickly looked away.

During the interval Tim suggested they have a cup of coffee. He told Claire to stay in her place while he fetched the drinks. As he walked off, she was reading the programme when a shadow loomed over her. She gasped when she saw Adam staring down at her, a mocking smile on his face.

'I see you're back in action, Claire. Is this another one of your fiancés? I believe he's a teacher at your school isn't he?'

'I . . . I . . er . . . '

'You don't have to explain anything to me. What you do is no concern of mine.'

'That's right.' Regaining her composure, anger took over. 'You're so self righteous,' she shrieked, turning to face him, 'And the most pompous man I've ever had the misfortune to meet. You're . . . '

'Hold on,' Adam interrupted.

Claire wouldn't stop, she was too wound up. 'I wanted to explain about Martin that day but you were so full of your own importance, you didn't even try to understand. Now you're jumping to false conclusions once again. Still, what does it matter? Anyone as arrogant as you would never listen to rational explanations. You can't believe you're ever wrong.' She ran out of steam and sat down, glancing around to see if they had been observed.

She was glad it was noisy in the church and no-one had been paying any attention to them.

'Just a minute, that's not fair,' Adam shouted.

'Fair! What a cheek!' She stood up, eyes blazing, ready to renew the attack.

'Becoming an inspector was the worst thing you ever did. It's gone to your head. Who on earth do you think you are?'

'I'm not listening to this. There's no point in talking to you when you're in this mood,' he snarled.

'Why did you talk to me?'

He was about to reply when a pretty young woman came up to them. 'Adam, there you are. I wondered where you were. I've got us some drinks. Can . . . ' she stopped suddenly aware that Adam and Claire were staring at each other. 'Oh, sorry, I didn't know you were talking to anyone. Can you take this please, Adam? It's very hot.' She passed him a coffee.

He took it, gave her a beaming smile and said, 'Thanks, Davina, you're a star. That's just what I need.'

'Aren't you going to introduce us, darling?' She looked at Claire.

'Er, Davina, this is Claire Robinson. I used to teach with her and I've just done an inspection at her school.

'Ooh, how nice. Pleased to meet you, Claire. I'm Adam's next door neighbour amongst other things,' she added smiling coyly at him. 'I hope he wasn't too hard on you. He can be a bit of a tyrant,' she laughed.

Claire shook the limp hand Davina offered, trying to hide her feelings of dismay. She glanced at Adam whose smile was still frozen on his face.

On the surface all traces of his previous anger had evaporated, but Claire could see his eyes gleaming like steel and a nerve which was throbbing in his neck.

'We get on so well, don't we, darling? Such good neighbours.' Davina smiled clutching a hold of Adam's hand possessively. 'Shall we go back to our seats now and have our drinks? Come on, Adam.' She playfully flicked back the lock of blond hair which had fallen across his forehead. 'You need to get your hair cut,' she said, kissing him on the cheek.

A Truce Is Called

Claire watched in horrified silence as Davina propelled Adam away. She observed that momentarily he looked annoyed, but then quickly regained his genial appearance and smiled down indulgently at the young woman.

They strode off holding hands without glancing back. She didn't even wait for me to reply, Claire thought. I've been dismissed by the pair of them.

Adam has the effrontery to criticise me for being with Tim, yet just a short time after he suggested we resume our relationship, he's carrying on with someone who's not much more than half his age. The ironic thing is that I only met Tim here by chance!

'Was that Adam Black I saw you talking to?' Tim enquired as he returned with their coffees, a puzzled expression on his face.

'That's right,' she murmured.

'He remembered you, then?'

'Yes.'

Had he heard their raised voices, Claire wondered? Did he suspect something? No, of course not, she was being paranoid. It was very noisy, he couldn't have heard.

Besides, Davina had seemed unaware of any tension between them, so there was no reason to think that Tim had noticed. A nagging voice in her head answered, 'He might have seen us while he was queuing up for the drinks'.

Well, did it matter if he had? He was just a friend and it was none of his business, but she needed her friends, especially now she was on her own.

'Claire? What do you think?'

'Sorry, I didn't hear what you said. It's so noisy in here.'

'I was just saying that gorgeous brunette with Adam Black looked almost young enough to be his daughter. I presume it's his wife. I must say I'm surprised.' He shook his head in disapproval.

Claire was trying to think of a reply but Tim continued, 'That young woman doesn't fit my image of an inspector's wife. Don't you agree?'

'Perhaps she's older than she looks. Anyway, what does an inspector's wife look like?' Claire was trying to defend Adam. Then she thought, why am I sticking up for him after what he's done?

She longed to tell Tim that Davina was not Adam's wife, but that would make everything worse. He would suspect something then. Instead, she changed the subject, 'This coffee's a bit strong.'

'Oh, shall I get you some more milk?'

'No. You'll have to queue up again. It's all right. It'll keep me awake for the second half of the concert.'

'You're not bored are you?'

'No, just a bit tired.'

'I still can't get over it,' Tim murmured.

247

'Get over what?'

'Adam Black's wife.'

'You're as bad as Sally.' Claire tried to lighten the situation.

'Why? What do you mean?'

'Referring to Adam Black's wife as gorgeous.'

'Oh, I see what you mean,' Tim smiled, 'but she is rather stunning.'

'That's what Sally said about Adam Black.'

'All right. I'll say no more. I don't want to make you jealous.'

'Tim!'

'Sorry. Let's change the subject.'

'A good idea.'

'But before we do, I'll just say I was surprised Adam recognised you and came over to speak. He sees so many teachers in his job. You must have made quite an impression on him.' Tim sipped his coffee thoughtfully.

'I expect he speaks to everyone he recognises.' Again she was defending Adam.

'I bet he doesn't remember them all.

I reckon he's a bit of a womaniser. You'd better watch out, Claire. I'm beginning to wonder if he's carrying on with that brunette while his wife is at home.'

'You don't know what you're talking about,' Claire snapped.

'Why? Do you know something I don't?'

'I thought we were changing the subject.'

'OK, but I haven't forgotten what Sally said.'

'What was that?' Claire's curiosity got the better of her.

'About you and Adam Black. She thought he was interested in you from the looks he was giving.'

'Don't be silly.' Claire blushed.

'I'll say no more now, but just heed my warning though. Anyway, it's nearly time for the second half. If you give me your cup I'll take it back before the music starts again.'

The concert resumed a few minutes later giving Claire an opportunity to ponder on the latest developments with Adam, which were whirring around in her head. At the end she realised she'd heard very little of the music.

'It was a brilliant concert, wasn't it?' Tim exclaimed as he applauded enthusiastically.

'Yes, lovely.'

'I'm so glad I came and meeting you here made it even better.'

Claire was too embarrassed to reply.

'I know I've said it before, but you look wonderful tonight. I love that colour you're wearing. Lilac, isn't it?'

'Yes,' she mumbled, her face flushed.

'How about having a drink with me? It's not very late.'

'No. Sorry, I'm tired. I wouldn't be good company.'

'You're always good company. I promise, it's just as friends. Please say you'll come. I won't keep you out too long.'

Claire was about to refuse when the thought struck her, why shouldn't I? I'm free, so is Tim. He's a friend.

There's no reason why we can't have a drink together. He knows I'm not in love with him. 'All right, I'll come.'

'Good. Shall we go in my car or walk?'

'It's a pleasant evening, let's walk. I won't be a moment.' Claire excused herself and hurried to the ladies' cloakroom.

She hoped that if they delayed long enough they would avoid meeting Adam and Davina. However, she was unlucky. Davina was coming out of the cloakroom and spotted Claire.

'Oh, hello, we meet again. It's Carla isn't it? You used to work with Adam many years ago?'

'No, I'm Claire actually,' she snapped, resenting the way Davina had implied that she must be getting on a bit if she knew Adam years ago.

'Sorry, I'm always making mistakes,' she laughed. 'Adam says it's because of my extreme youth.'

Claire found Davina very irritating. Whatever does he see in her she wondered? I know she's pretty but that's all. She doesn't seem very engaging. Then she felt guilty for thinking that.

'I'd better go and find Adam,' Davina was saying. 'He'll be getting impatient for me.' She smiled conspiratorially at Claire and added, 'He's such a catch. Charming and intelligent. I can't believe my good luck in finding him.' She paused for breath. 'I know he's a bit older than me but that's what makes him interesting. Anyway got to go. Bye, Carl, er, Claire.'

Davina walked away and Claire had to hold onto the wash basin to steady herself. She gripped it tightly thinking, I could throttle that woman, or rather, girl. After all that's what she is a very silly little girl.

Adam must be mad to get involved with her, but isn't it your own fault? She asked herself. Adam probably only turned to Davina because of the misunderstanding he had with you over Martin. Claire tried to banish this thought from her mind. There was nothing she could do about that now. Slowly she made her way back to Tim.

'You were a long time,' he commented. 'Are you all right?' He scrutinised her flushed face.

'Sorry to keep you waiting. I was talking to someone.'

'It doesn't matter. Let's go. I've just seen Adam Black and that girl again. I wonder if she is his wife.'

★　★　★

The rest of the evening passed pleasantly. Tim was good company and Claire tried to be responsive to him. When they returned to the car park Tim said, 'I have enjoyed myself. We should do this again.'

'You'll be busy with the ramblers. I'm surprised you weren't with them this evening.'

'I wanted to go to the concert instead and I'm very glad I did.'

Claire was still intrigued to know

whether Tim had known that she was going to the concert, but decided it was better to say no more about it.

'Why don't you come on a ramble too? We don't do anything too strenuous and I'm sure Sally would be pleased to see you.'

'She wouldn't even notice. She's too wrapped up in Grant.'

'You may be right about that. But I'd like it if you came. Think about it, Claire.'

'It's not really my thing, the great outdoors. Goodnight, Tim. Thanks for the drink.' She opened the door of her car, quickly jumped in and drove off.

One evening Claire decided she needed a break from school work so she was relaxing, enjoying the luxury of reading a romantic novel instead of frantically preparing for the next day's lessons, when the telephone rang. She wasn't expecting a call so guessed it was her sister, wanting to find out how she was. Claire picked up the receiver and cheerfully said, 'Hello,' She nearly dropped it when she recognised the voice at the other end.

'How are you, Claire?'

She sat down clutching the armchair for support, her heart hammering in her chest. 'Adam? Why are you ringing me?'

'That's not very welcoming.'

'Should I be?'

'Perhaps not,' he conceded. 'We didn't part on very good terms.'

'That's putting it mildly,' Claire answered sarcastically.

'You're right.'

'So, what do you want?'

'I was going to apologise for walking out on you that day.'

'It's a bit late for that.'

'What do you mean?'

'I don't think Davina will be very pleased.'

'Don't worry about her.'

'That's not very nice.'

'Forget Davina. I don't want to talk about her.'

'It's always what you want,' Claire

blurted out. 'Davina's your girlfriend.'

'She's not.'

'Oh, so you've ditched her?'

'No, she, she's,' Adam hesitated. 'She's with someone else.'

'And that's why you're ringing me?' Claire was scornful. 'She's ditched you, so you want a shoulder to cry on. Well, you've come to the wrong person.'

'Of course that's not the reason I rang you. Listen Claire, I don't intend to start another argument. I wanted to apologise and I was going to suggest we meet up again. Then I could explain things properly. There's a lot we need to talk about. What do you say, Claire? You've gone very quiet.'

Her heart was racing. Adam wanted to see her again. Should she agree? She felt tempted, but at the back of her mind she kept picturing him with Davina. 'I don't know,' she prevaricated.

'Why? Because you're seeing Tim Harding, is that it? You took up with him pretty quickly, or were you seeing him all along?'

'No,' she shouted. 'There you go again, accusing me of all sorts of things without knowing any of the facts. You say we need to talk, but we don't talk, we just argue.'

'Claire, I, I'm,' he interrupted.

'Let me finish, Adam. You have the effrontery to mention Tim, who for your information has never been more than a friend, yet you've been carrying on with Davina.' She clenched and unclenched her fist. 'Someone,' she continued, 'who, who's nearly young enough to be your daughter.'

'Claire, if you'll let me speak.'

'Go on then, but what excuses can there be?' she muttered running out of steam.

'Davina and I have not been carrying on, as you put it.'

'It looked like it to me.'

'She's not as young as she looks,' Adam went on, ignoring Claire's comment. 'And I'm not quite old enough to be her father, even if some days I feel it.'

Claire's conscience pricked her. She was remembering the terrible things that had happened to Adam. 'Sorry.'

'Well, what's your answer, can we meet?'

'Er, I suppose we can.'

'Don't sound so enthusiastic!'

'Should I be?'

'I won't answer that. Are you free on Saturday evening?'

'I think so.'

'There's a good restaurant in Springwood. We could have dinner if you like. That would give us a chance to talk. What do you say?'

'All right.'

'I'll pick you up at seven. Goodbye Claire, and try to calm down before Saturday. It's not good for your blood pressure, getting so het up.'

Claire slammed the phone down, her emotions churning. Although she wanted to see Adam again, and hoped that this time they would talk, his sarcasm infuriated her. He never used to be like that, she mused, he was always so easy going, but after what he's been through, I suppose it isn't surprising. Even now she found herself defending Adam.

On Saturday Claire spent a long time deciding what to wear. She didn't want to look over-dressed, but on the other hand she didn't want to be too casual.

After all, Adam was now an inspector and probably frequented more lavish restaurants than when he was younger. Finally Claire selected a peach crêpe two-piece which she had recently purchased on a lonely shopping trip when she'd been feeling particularly depressed. At the time she'd wondered when she would wear it. This seemed an appropriate occasion.

At precisely seven o'clock the door-bell rang. Claire peeped through the window and saw Adam looking immaculate in a navy suit.

She was glad she'd made an effort and put on her peach outfit. As she opened the door she could feel her heart beating madly.

'Hello, Claire. It's good to see you.'

She gazed up, noting his vivid green

eyes and the blond curls which were falling around his forehead. He's grown his hair longer, she thought. I always preferred it that way.

Adam hesitantly took hold of Claire's hand and led her to his car. She moved as if in a dream. She stepped into his large grey Rover, feeling as nervous as a schoolgirl. Will I ever grow up, Claire wondered? I'm nearly thirty, it's time I did.

They were quiet for most of the journey. Claire sat rigid to stop herself from trembling. Occasionally she glanced at Adam's face as he drove. His expression was inscrutable. She was desperately trying to think of something interesting to say. In the end they both started speaking at once and then stopped abruptly.

'After you,' Adam said.

'I was just thinking what a lovely evening it is,' Claire murmured, 'Sunny and warm.'

'Yes, the weather's fine for early June.'

Suddenly Adam burst out laughing.

Claire looked at him in astonishment. 'What's so funny?'

'We are,' he replied still chuckling.

'Why?'

'Well, you must see the funny side of it.'

'What do you mean?'

'We haven't met since that awful day when I walked out on you, yet all we can talk about is the weather.'

'We met at the concert,' Claire pointed out petulantly. 'Or have you forgotten? You know the one you went to with Davina.'

'I don't count that as meeting. We just bumped into each other there.'

'Oh.' Claire was spared from saying anything else as they were turning into the restaurant car park. She'd been right. It was very smart.

Adam escorted her inside. She looked around at her fellow guests. They were all elegantly attired. She felt pleased that she was wearing her new suit. The manager greeted them and showed them to a candlelit table discretely positioned in a secluded alcove next to a window.

When they were seated Adam said, 'You look charming tonight, Claire. That colour really suits you.'

'Thank you.' She was annoyed to feel herself blushing.

The waiter appeared with the menu. As she studied it, Adam ordered the drinks. He's remembered what I like she thought. Finally after making their choices he asked, 'Now can we get back to how we were before I walked out on you?'

'I don't know. A lot has happened since then.'

'Has it?'

'Yes.'

'Tell me about it.'

'You and Davina to start with.'

'Claire, when I rang to apologise, I told you there was nothing going on between Davina and myself.'

'That's not what I saw at the concert.'

'Look Claire, I only went out with

Davina because I was upset and annoyed with you. I thought we were finished for good.'

'So you used Davina. I'm surprised at you, Adam. I'm even beginning to feel sorry for her.'

'I'm not proud of what I did, but I was in a state over you and Davina was there, young, attractive and eager to go out with me.'

'And you couldn't resist?'

'What man would?'

The waiter brought their drinks. Both kept quiet until he'd walked away.

'A man who really had feelings for someone else wouldn't immediately rush off with the first person on offer,' Claire stated testily.

'He might if he thought those feelings were hopeless.'

'Poor Davina,' Claire murmured.

'Don't feel too sorry for her. She's quite happy. Found someone her own age. She was never seriously interested in me. I think she just liked the idea of going out with an older man.'

'And you were flattered that someone so young found you attractive?'

'I suppose so. I am human you know. After Beth died,' Adam went on, 'I was lonely and miserable.' He paused and Claire felt guilty again.

He'd suffered greatly. She glanced at him but he was staring at the table seemingly unaware of her confusion.

'Then meeting you again,' he continued, 'I hoped that we could get back together, but when I found out you were engaged, I just couldn't handle it.'

'I'm sorry,' she whispered.

'I was in such a state of depression,' he added, 'that when Davina moved next door and threw herself at me, I gave in and went along with it.'

'Until she got fed up with you?'

'That's right. I knew it would never work, so I wasn't upset when she finished with me. I was actually quite relieved.'

Suddenly Claire smiled, remembering what her colleagues had said. 'Sally and Tim thought Davina was your wife.'

'And you told them she wasn't?' He looked up at her.

'No, I didn't say anything even though I was tempted to.'

'I don't know which was worse, them believing she was my wife, or you thinking she was my girlfriend.'

'They were shocked. Tim warned me to beware of you. He said you might be a womaniser.' Claire giggled.

'The cheek!' Adam smiled too. Then he added, 'Last week I made a few decisions.'

'What were they?'

'Well, the first was to try and sort things out with you.'

'And the second?'

'I'll tell you that later.'

'Are there any more?'

'One, but I'll leave that for now too.'

'You're getting me intrigued.'

'Good. Now I think we should enjoy our meal and leave any serious discussion until afterwards.'

The waiter placed their starters on the table. The food was excellent. Claire surprised herself by having a hearty appetite. She had feared she'd be too nervous to enjoy the meal, but gradually she relaxed and felt quite at ease. Her heart was no longer racing and she was calm and composed.

They chatted companionably about school and Adam's latest inspection. Finally, when they were drinking coffee, both having eaten, nervously, he said, 'Now you can tell me about your fiancé.'

'There's not a lot to tell. I sort of drifted into the engagement. I liked Martin, but I should never have agreed to marry him. We weren't suited.'

'Why?'

'We wanted different things from life. He didn't understand about teaching, how it takes over your whole life. He used to get annoyed when I brought work of an evening and couldn't spend time with him.

'When Martin phoned me I was often doing school work and couldn't talk for long. He told me to just leave it.

He didn't understand that I couldn't.'

'Other people do find that hard to believe.'

'Anyway, Martin kept asking me to marry him and in the end I gave in. Then soon afterwards I saw you again and realised that I shouldn't have given in. I didn't love him enough.'

'And was that why you broke it off with me, Claire? You didn't love me enough?' Adam stared intently at her.

'No. That was not the reason. It was all so stupid. I know that now, but at the time I, I ... ' she twisted the serviette round and round in her hand, a look of anguish on her face. 'Oh Adam, this isn't the time or the place to talk about it,' she sighed.

'All right.' He patted her hand. 'But will you tell me one day? Please, Claire?'

'I'll try.'

'I'm sorry I interrupted. Please go on.'

'I broke off the engagement with Martin the day before you came to lunch at my flat. I had no idea that he'd turn up there. It wasn't the sort of thing he did. He was very precise and predictable. He always made arrangements and stuck to them. He never acted on the spur of the moment.'

'But he did that day.'

'Yes, and with devastating consequences. You wouldn't listen to my explanation.'

'No. I'm sorry Claire, but I was so shocked at seeing Martin that I didn't think straight.' Adam took hold of her hands. 'I'm glad you've told me about him. If only I had listened that day, all these weeks of misery could have been avoided.'

'Well, at least you know now. Also while we're clearing the air, I'd like to point out that it was by chance I met Tim at the concert. We're just friends and work colleagues. There's never been anything between us.'

'But he'd like there to be?'

'Yes,' Claire murmured, still holding Adam's hands as she gazed enquiringly up at him. 'But how did you know or were you just guessing?'

'I could see it in his eyes.'

'Oh.' She didn't know what else to say.

Adam removed his hands from Claire's, looked at his watch and said, 'I think we'd better go. Do you realise we've been sitting here for three hours?'

He paid the bill and they returned to his car. Claire sank back into its luxurious interior, feeling happy and full. The evening had gone well. After the tricky start they'd regained their old relaxed attitude with each other.

When they reached her flat he escorted her to the door then bent down, gently kissed her forehead and walked away without looking back, leaving Claire staring after him, a bemused expression on her face.

A Strange Farewell

Claire lay in bed reliving the events of the evening. It had gone so well until the end. She wondered why Adam hadn't said anything further?

He had kissed her though only a gentle kiss such as you might give to a friend. But that's all we are, she reminded herself, friends. Now you're the one trying to rush things.

She'd criticised Martin for doing that and yet here she was doing the same thing with Adam. Besides, she couldn't blame him for being cautious after what happened all those years ago. There was something else niggling her too. He hadn't suggested another date or even said he would get in touch.

Had he regretted going out with her? She'd been thinking that everything had gone well but maybe he didn't agree. Perhaps he was wary of her. On the other hand, he was the one who rang to apologise. She didn't know what to make of it all. These thoughts went whirling round in her head causing her to have another sleepless night.

Claire spent the following day preparing for her return to school. She felt tired and irritable but was annoyed with herself for doing so. She hoped that Adam would ring, but he didn't and she was determined that she wouldn't telephone him. She would wait for him to make the next move.

On Monday at school Tim enquired about her half term holiday. 'It was restful,' she told him.

'That doesn't sound very exciting,' he replied.

'No, but I needed a break. What did you do?'

'I went out with the ramblers a couple of times. You should have come. It would have done you good. Lots of fresh air, friendly company, it might have put some colour in your cheeks.'

'Did Sally go?'

'Yes, but I hardly saw her. She was much too busy with Grant.'

'I should have guessed,' Claire laughed.

That evening Elizabeth telephoned from Scotland. 'I'll be glad when this baby arrives,' she told Claire. 'I'm getting so big I can hardly move. I don't know what I'll be like in a month's time.'

'Are you sure you're not having twins?' Claire asked.

'Definitely not! I've had the scan but the doctor wonders if I've got my dates right. He said I should be prepared for the baby to come early.'

'Oh, I hope I've broken up from school by the time it's born.'

'Don't worry if you haven't. My friend, Sara, has agreed to help me out. She can't wait. I've promised her she can be an honorary aunt. She adores children, but she's never married and now she's in her forties, she doubts that she'll ever have a child of her own. She's really going to spoil my little one.'

'I'm glad you've got Sara. You do understand that I can't just leave school in the middle of term and come up to Edinburgh?'

'Of course I know that. Don't worry about me. We'll cope. Anyway, the doctor might be wrong, but the way I feel now I hope the baby will arrive sooner. I just can't get comfortable. I forgot to tell you, Brian's bought me a new mobile phone and he's going to teach me how to text. You'll soon be fed up with receiving texts from me.'

'You are getting with it,' Claire laughed.

After chatting for a few more minutes, she hung up, intending to do some marking but the telephone rang almost immediately. She picked up the receiver thinking it was Elizabeth again, but it was Adam's voice she heard.

'Hello Claire. I've been trying to get you for ages. I was beginning to think your phone was out of order.'

'I was talking to my sister, Elizabeth. She's expecting a baby. It's due next month but she was telling me that the doctor thinks it could be sooner.'

'Good for her! You'll be an auntie. Lucky thing! I wish I'd had a brother or sister. Being an only child can be lonely.

'Do you still see Beth's parents?' Claire asked tentatively.

'Yes, about once a month. They've aged so much.'

'I don't suppose you ever get over something like that.'

'No, you don't, but I didn't ring up to discuss my problems. I wondered if I could call in one evening for a chat and a cup of coffee? I've started an inspection this week and there's a lot of paperwork to do, but I need a break now and then. And ... ' Adam hesitated, 'It would give us a chance to get to know one another again, see how things go. What do you say?'

'I'd love it.' Claire couldn't conceal the delight she was feeling. Her heart was racing. Adam wanted to see her again. 'What about Wednesday?' she asked.

'That'll be fine. I'll come at about nine if that's not too late. It'll give me a chance to do some work first.'

After he'd hung up Claire's mood improved enormously as it did in school for the next two days.

'You look happy,' Tim remarked on Wednesday morning.

'Well, there's no point in being miserable. You've got to make the most of your life.'

'My sentiments exactly, so how about coming out with me on Saturday? There's a good film on at the Ritz.'

'No. I don't think so.'

'Why? He asked. 'You don't agree there's a good film on, or you don't want my company?'

'Tim, I've explained before why I won't go out with you.' Will he ever give up? Claire thought.

'And I've told you we'll just be friends.'

'It wouldn't work. Please don't keep on at me.'

'All right I'll go on my own then.'

'You could find someone else to take.'

'I don't want to,' Tim replied.

Claire quickly changed the conversation by telling him about an incident that had occurred in her classroom the previous day.

The evening seemed to drag on and on while Claire was waiting for Adam to arrive. She'd eaten dinner, finished her school work, showered and changed into a pretty summer dress. It had been a scorching hot day and she was glad she'd recently purchased an electric fan.

She switched it on and sat back enjoying the feel of the cool air blowing on her face. Claire wasn't sure if it was the weather or the prospect of spending the evening with Adam which was making her feel so restless.

At a quarter past nine she was wondering if he had changed his mind and wasn't coming. When the telephone rang she picked it up expecting to hear Adam's voice but it was Martin instead.

'I was worried and wanted to find out how you were,' he said. 'It's so long since I've spoken to you.'

'I'm fine thank you. How are you?' she enquired, wishing he hadn't picked this precise moment to phone her. Claire didn't want Adam to arrive and find her speaking to Martin on the telephone. She was frantically trying to think up a way of getting rid of him. 'I'm sorry I'll have to go. I'm expecting someone'.

She put down the phone as she heard the doorbell ringing.

Claire flew to the door, opened it breathlessly and looked up at Adam's face. He was giving her the same devastating smile that she remembered so well.

'You're out of breath,' he murmured taking hold of her hands. 'You didn't have to run to the door. I'm glad you're so eager to see me of course, but I could have waited you know.'

'Claire flushed, feeling foolish. She looked away and said, 'I was on the telephone and didn't want to get involved in a long conversation, so I hung up. That was why I rushed to the door,' she finished primly.

'I hope whoever it was, wasn't offended. You shouldn't have rung off on my account.'

'No, it's quite all right. It was Martin.' Claire pulled her hands away from his. 'Are you going to come inside?'

'Thanks. I was beginning to think we were going to spend all the evening standing here on your doorstep.' Adam followed her into the lounge.

'Sit down. I'll make some coffee.'

'Claire,' He came towards her.

'Yes,' she breathed.

'Don't go away.'

'I was going to put the kettle on.'

'It can wait.' Adam stood in front gazing down at her. Suddenly his arms encircled Claire, his eyes never leaving hers, as she stared at him incredulously.

Then he kissed her lips very gently at first, waiting to see what her reaction would be. Tentatively she put her arms around him as if she were in a dream. Was this really happening? His kisses became increasingly more passionate and Claire found herself responding with equal fervour. All her pent up feelings of longing for him which had been stifled for so many years, surfaced and she was kissing him with an intensity that surprised even her.

After a few minutes Adam pulled away saying, 'It's like we've turned back the clock.'

Claire felt her face getting even redder as she mumbled, 'I'll put the kettle on.'

She hurried into the kitchen, shocked and embarrassed by her abandoned behaviour. I shouldn't have kissed him like that she thought. I should have been more restrained. Where's my self control?

Claire switched the kettle on and leaned against the wall trying to pull herself together. Her hand was still shaking as she poured the coffee.

She took a deep breath and carried the drinks into the lounge where Adam was sitting on one of the armchairs flicking through a newspaper, looking perfectly calm and composed. There was no trace of the passion he'd displayed a few minutes earlier.

'Thank you, Claire. That's just what I need,' he said as she placed the cups on the table along with a plate of cakes.

She sat opposite Adam on the sofa sipping her drink, not daring to look at him, unaware that he was watching her intently. Neither spoke. She was feeling too overwhelmed by the emotion she had displayed.

At last Adam said, 'That kiss has just confirmed to me how much I still care for you, Claire. It felt so right to have you back in my arms again.'

She looked away flushing with embarrassment once more.

'I'm not intending to upset or annoy you, I'm just attempting to understand.'

'What are you trying to understand?' Claire interrupted.

'The fact that obviously you still have some feelings for me, even though all those years ago you abandoned me so suddenly. You do have feelings for me. I'm right, aren't I?'

'Yes,' she whispered.

Adam fixed his gaze on her. 'Good. Please Claire, will you explain what really happened? Why did you break off our engagement?'

'Oh, Adam,' she sighed. 'It's not easy.'

'Please try. There'll never be a better time to tell me.'

He moved over to the sofa and sat down beside her, gently putting his arm around her shoulder.

He was right about that. It was now or never. She knew he wouldn't be happy when he heard what she had to say, but he had a right to know. Afterwards he might not want to have any more to do with her but it was a risk she had to take. She gulped, took a deep breath and started, 'I acted too hastily. I . . . '

'Go on, Claire. Don't stop now.' He squeezed her hand.

She closed her eyes as if trying to blot out the memory, fighting back the tears which threatened to come. 'I don't think I can do this,' she choked.

'Yes you can. Look at me, Claire. I need to know what happened. There's no way forward for either of us unless everything's out in the open.'

She knew he was right. She had to go on. She owed it to Adam. She began quietly, 'You remember I had to go to Cyprus to look after my mother.'

'Of course I do,' Adam interrupted. 'She was very ill and you gave up your job in England to look after her. I'm not likely to forget. It was after that you finished with me. Did you think I wouldn't wait for you to come back?'

'Let me continue.'

'Sorry. Go on.'

'Well, I came home a few days earlier than I'd planned. My mother seemed to be getting on quite well so I decided to give you a surprise.'

'I didn't know. When was this?'

'I'm trying to tell you,' Claire groaned. 'You're not making it easy.'

'All right. I'll keep quiet.' Adam released Claire and sat back on the sofa.

You won't be quiet in a minute, Claire thought, when you hear what I have to say. 'I . . . I was feeling happy and excited and couldn't wait to see you again so I came round to your house but as I approached your front door,' Claire stifled a sob, remembering the pain she'd felt all those years ago. 'You were kissing someone else, a tall blonde woman. You didn't see me, you were so wrapped up in her.'

'Oh Claire,' Adam's face had turned pale. 'You've got it all wrong. I didn't do that.'

'I just turned round and ran home,' she continued, seeming unaware of his remark. 'I couldn't believe you'd do that behind my back while I was away looking after my mother. I'd trusted you and you'd betrayed me. I couldn't forgive you for that. That was why I finished with you.'

'It was a long time ago, but I'm quite sure I wasn't kissing anyone,' Adam replied indignantly.' I would never have done that.'

'But I saw you.'

'I don't know what you thought you were seeing, but I definitely wasn't kissing anyone.'

'So I'm making this up?' Claire snorted.

'No, I'm not saying that but I think you were mistaken. Oh my goodness, I've just remembered. A tall, blonde woman. That was Lydia Barclay. She was a teacher at my school. She was newly widowed and feeling very lonely. Some of us were trying to help. If you hadn't run away you would have seen that I wasn't on my own with her. Yes, I recall it quite clearly. There was a group of us. We'd all been out for lunch together and stopped off at my house for coffee. She left to go home before the others so I went to the door to see her off.

'But you were kissing her,' Claire murmured.'

'No, I remember being somewhat surprised when she threw her arms around me and kissed me, but she was just saying thank you for a lovely time. That's all it was Claire, nothing more. If you'd come in you would have seen the others. They were still there.'

'But, I'd heard . . . '

'What did you hear?

'Someone wrote to me in Cyprus saying they thought I ought to know they'd seen you.'

'Go on.' Adam tapped his foot impatiently.

'They'd seen you with a tall, blonde girl.'

'Yes. That was Lydia.'

'You don't deny it? Adam you were engaged to me. What were you doing with her?'

'I told you. She'd just lost her husband. I gave her a lift a couple of times. I felt sorry for her. I was trying to help. I'd no idea anyone would misconstrue the situation. Who was it that told you? I hope they realise the mischief they've caused.'

'It doesn't matter now who it was.'

'I can't believe that's what made you break off our engagement. You didn't give me a chance to explain. You shouted down the phone at me when I rang and implied that I should know what was wrong. How could I if you didn't tell me? If only you'd told me what you'd seen everything could have been so different.'

'I know that now,' Claire whispered. 'I should have asked what was going on, but seeing you with this Lydia woman made me think that there must be some truth in the letter. I'd ignored it at first, dismissed it out of hand, not wanting to believe what it said, but when I saw you kissing Lydia I thought it must be true.'

'You had so little trust in me you believed some mischief maker and condemned me out of hand without hearing my side of the story.' Adam banged his fist on the table. 'How could you do that? I was your fiancé. We were going to be married.'

'I'm sorry,' Claire whispered.

'You completely misjudged me. I don't know if I can forget that.'

'What else can I say?'

'I don't know. If you'd just tried to explain I could have told you about Lydia. I'd no idea that you were upset about her. I racked my brain trying to think of anything I could have done to offend you, but in the end I gave up. I kept telling myself if that was the way you treated me I was better off without you. I even thought that maybe you'd met someone else in Cyprus.'

'How could you think that?'

'I didn't know what to think. I still don't understand why you wouldn't let me explain though.'

'I suppose my pride was hurt. Seeing you with Lydia, was such a shock to my system I couldn't bring myself to trust you again. I think I'd built you up in my mind to be some sort of super hero and

I felt let down so I wouldn't listen to anything you said.'

'But I was your fiancé,' Adam repeated.

'I know,' Claire interrupted, 'you don't need to remind me. I was completely in the wrong and I've paid the penalty for it.'

'I kept ringing and leaving messages but you never replied,' Adam murmured. 'I just didn't know what to do.'

'I was so angry I wanted to punish you for what you'd done.'

'But I hadn't done anything. I was devastated.'

'I'm so sorry,' Claire groaned. 'I don't know what excuse I can make except that I was young and foolish. I should have listened to you.'

'Yes you should and then years of anguish could have been avoided,' Adam said bitterly.

'Please. I realised all this too late.'

'So you went back to Cyprus?'

'Yes. I decided to get a job. After all my parents had a holiday home there so it seemed the sensible thing to do. They were upset about our broken engagement and said I could stay as long as I liked. They didn't try to influence me in any way.'

'So they thought I was being unfaithful to you?'

'No. I just told them I'd changed my mind. I never once mentioned what I'd seen. I suppose I was too proud.' Claire's voice became a whisper. 'I suppose I didn't want anyone to think that you'd been cheating on me'

'I hadn't,' Adam shouted.

'I'm sorry. I know that now, but I didn't then.'

'You should have trusted me,' Adam repeated.

'I realised that when it was too late.'

'What do you mean?'

'One day I had a phone call from my friend, Jessica. Do you remember her?'

'Yes I think so.'

'We were having a chat about old times when Jessica asked me if I knew you had moved. It seems that one of our friends had mentioned it to her. She said that you'd been heartbroken at what happened and had tried to contact me. By then I'd gradually calmed down and realised I should have confronted you with my suspicions instead of running away. I knew then that I'd misjudged you. I asked her if she knew your new address but she didn't. I'd left it too late. I was so upset, but there was nothing more I could do.'

'Well,' Adam replied, 'after you'd ignored all my phone calls and not answered any of my letters, I decided to get another job. I was lucky I found one quickly so I moved away. I wanted to make a fresh start.'

'And that's what I did, in Cyprus,' Claire continued. 'I had to rebuild my life.'

'Yet when we met again you agreed to see me?'

'I don't think you would have taken no for an answer.'

'You're right, I wouldn't have. Seeing you again brought all the old feelings to the surface. I had to have one final attempt at discovering what went wrong, but I couldn't do anything until the inspection was out of the way. It was agonising waiting all those months.'

'It was for me too. I was in such a muddle, engaged to Martin yet constantly thinking about you, regretting my actions.'

Adam took hold of Claire's hands and gazed into her eyes. 'Now do you believe that nothing was ever going on between me and Lydia?'

'Yes, I do,' she breathed, gazing up at him, hoping that he would kiss her again.

'Good. I'm glad that's out of the way at last.' Suddenly Adam pulled his hands away and looked at his watch. 'It's time I went home. I've some serious thinking to do. Goodnight, Claire.' He walked to the door and let himself out leaving her staring disconsolately after him.

A New Life

Claire spent another sleepless night when Adam had gone. She was glad that everything was out in the open at last but was worried about his abrupt departure. He said he had some serious thinking to do. Did that mean he wasn't sure of his feelings? Or was he unable to forgive her for leaving him?

Claire found it hard to concentrate at school the next day and was glad when home time came. She hadn't been in very long when the telephone rang.

'Claire, it's Adam. Can I call round again this evening? I think we need to continue our conversation. You're not too busy are you?'

'No, just the usual marking to be done, that's all.'

'I'll come about nine if that's OK?'

'Lovely. I'll see you then.'

Claire hung up not knowing what to

think. In one way she was glad that Adam was coming round, but she was also very worried. This was going to be a momentous evening. Their futures hung in the balance. Either they would continue seeing each other or they would finally finish. There could be no other outcome.

When Adam arrived he kissed her briefly on the cheek. 'It's good to see you, Claire.'

'Come and sit down,' she urged. 'I'll make the coffee.'

'Thanks. I could do with some. It's been a hard day.'

Claire walked into the kitchen with a sinking heart. Adam had displayed no emotion at all. She'd no idea what he was thinking. Had he come to some decision? Was he going to finish with her? If he did, it would be no more than she deserved. She quickly made the drinks and nervously carried them into the lounge where Adam was sitting with his eyes closed.

As she placed them on the table he

opened them and said very formally, 'Thank you, Claire.'

They sat drinking, no-one speaking a word. Claire was desperately trying to think of something to say. She glanced up and saw that Adam was staring down as if he was lost in thought. She couldn't help thinking that he was still as attractive as the day she had first set eyes on him. In spite of all the troubles he had experienced, his appearance hadn't deteriorated at all. In fact, it was even better, quite distinguished looking.

Finally he placed his cup on the table and said, 'That was delicious.'

'Good. Would you like another?'

'Later please. Claire, I've been thinking.'

What was he going to say? Was he going to end it all? He looked so serious. 'Yes?' she looked at him expectantly.

'There aren't any more secrets I need to know are there, Claire?' He looked up at her.

'No, Adam. There's nothing else.'

'And do you believe that there never was anything going on between me and Lydia?'

'Yes, I told you yesterday. I'm sorry I was such a silly, suspicious young girl. I should have known better.'

'Then in that case can we continue seeing each other? What do you say?'

'Oh, Adam,' she gasped. 'You've forgiven me?'

'Yes, of course. What else could I do? So what's your answer, Claire? Can we continue seeing each other?'

'Yes. That's what I want. I've been dreaming of it so long.'

'You have?' He looked astounded.

'Surely you realised?'

'No. After what happened before I didn't dare . . .'

'You still don't trust me?' Claire interrupted.

'To be honest, I just don't know, but I want to.'

'Then I will have to prove that I'm a different person. I'm grown up now, Adam. I think before I act. I was young and stupid then.'

'All right, wise one.'

Claire laughed and Adam joined in too. 'Shall I make another coffee?'

'Please. I'd love one. What about a kiss first?'

'Later,' she said seriously. 'We've some more talking to do.'

'We have?'

'Yes. You stay there. I won't be long.'

Claire almost skipped to the kitchen. Everything was going so well. All her fears about Adam wanting to finish with her had been groundless. He'd forgiven her. She quickly replenished their cups, took them into the lounge, placed them on the table and sat down beside Adam.

'I can't believe we're actually sitting here doing this,' he suddenly said.

'We're only drinking coffee,' Claire laughed. 'There's nothing remarkable in that.'

'You know what I mean.'

'I do. I feel the same way. I thought this was never going to happen.'

'All those wasted years!' Adam exclaimed.

'Don't call them wasted. You had Beth then. You gave her some happiness in her tragically short life. If you'd been with me, she wouldn't have had that happiness.'

'You don't know that. She might have found someone else.'

'And she might not. Let's look to the future now. We can't change the past.'

'You're so unselfish, Claire.' He took her hands in his.

'I'm not really,' she protested. 'I'm just trying to be realistic. Adam . . . you told me the other day that you had made three decisions. I know the first one was to sort things out with me. Well, we seem to have done that, so what were the other two?'

'I'll tell you the second, but you'll have to wait for another time to hear the third.'

'That sounds intriguing. Now you're teasing me,' Claire smiled thinking this is more like the old Adam.

'That's my insurance policy to make sure you keep on seeing me. I know what a curious mind you have. I'll enjoy keeping you guessing.' He laughed and Claire playfully threw a cushion at him.

'What was the second decision?'

'I'm giving up my job as an Ofsted inspector. I'm going back to being a head teacher.'

'Brilliant! But why? I thought you were quite settled. I never imagined I'd hear that.'

'I think I've done my bit for Ofsted. Now it's time for someone else to have a go. I hope I've been fair and done a good job.'

'I'm sure you have. We all thought so at my school. Have you found a new post yet?'

'Yes, I'm starting in September as Head of Springwood Primary School.'

'Ooh that's lovely. I'm so glad Adam. I was beginning to worry that you might be moving away back to London.'

'No, I like it much better here. Besides . . . '

Adam didn't get a chance to finish the sentence as the telephone rang. Claire groaned. This always happened at the most inopportune moments. 'I'll let it ring and listen to the answerphone later.'

'No,' Adam replied, 'it might be important.'

'All right.' Claire picked up the receiver. 'Hello.'

'It's Brian. I've some good news for you. Liz has had her baby. You're an auntie!'

'What already?' she gasped. 'Is Liz OK?'

'Fine, and the baby too. You've got a little niece. They're both doing well.'

'That's wonderful. I can't believe it. She wasn't due for another month, was she?'

'No. I think we must have got the dates wrong.'

'Liz had said that to me but I wasn't expecting it yet. I was hoping it would

299

be in my school holidays. Still, the important thing is that they're both all right. Is her friend, Sara, able to come and help?'

'Yes, and I'm having a couple of weeks off work so we'll manage. You don't have to worry.'

Claire mouthed to Adam, 'I'm an auntie.'

He came over and put his arms around her as she continued to chat to her brother-in-law. When she'd hung up Claire said, 'I can't wait to see them. I forgot to ask the weight of the baby and if they'd chosen a name yet.'

'Why don't you go this weekend or the following one? You could travel on Friday night and return on Sunday evening. You could fly there. I'll look up some flights for you if you like. There are a lot of bargains around at the moment.'

'I suppose I could.'

'You should. It's not every day that you become an auntie. I do envy you. I'd love to have nephews and nieces.'

Suddenly Claire felt sad remembering the great loss Adam had suffered, but he was smiling, pleased at her good fortune. She was easily persuaded and decided to go the following week.

'That will give Brian and Liz time to get themselves sorted before I descend upon them,' she told Adam.

'Good,' he replied. 'Then I can see you again this weekend.'

When Adam finally left her flat that night, Claire was much too excited to sleep. She kept thinking back over all the events of the evening and the long lingering kiss Adam had given her before he hurried off.

Thoughts about Liz and the baby were also filling her mind. What a day this has been she said to herself! I don't think I have ever been so happy. Well, maybe that day years ago when Adam and I got engaged was an equally happy one, she amended.

A Past Forgotten

Claire spent the next Saturday with Adam. It was a scorching hot day and they took a picnic to a nearby village. From the moment he arrived at her flat to collect her, they were perfectly at ease with one another.

It was as if the last few years had never happened and they were back to their old relationship. Claire was bursting with happiness and Adam seemed more like his former self. Nothing else was said about the past and they just enjoyed their day together.

When it was finally time for them to part Claire kissed Adam passionately, clinging to him, not wanting to let go. 'We've got the rest of our lives before us. It won't hurt to be apart for a while,' he said.

Claire liked the sound of those words. Would it all work out this time?

Dare she hope that soon they would be together permanently? Then a little voice in her head whispered, you've only just started seeing Adam again. Don't rush things. That's what Martin did, rushed everything and that didn't work out. You don't want to make the same mistake.

But this is different, she told herself. I've never stopped loving Adam. I don't think I truly loved Martin.

★ ★ ★

At school that week, Claire walked around in a happy daze. She noticed Tim looking at her quizzically. 'I've become an auntie,' she informed him.

'Congratulations,' he replied.

She hoped he would think that was the reason she was so cheerful. She wasn't going to tell anyone about her relationship with Adam yet, it was much too soon.

The next weekend Claire stayed with her sister in Edinburgh. She was delighted with her little niece, Melissa, and almost felt sorry when she had to return home. Adam sent her text messages late each evening and she'd managed to ring him a couple of times when Elizabeth was busy with the baby.

'You look very well,' her sister commented, noting the light, golden tan Claire had acquired.

'It's the sunshine and being an auntie. I love spending time with Melissa. She's gorgeous.'

'Maybe you'll have a baby yourself one day.'

'Ooh, I don't know about that,' Claire answered, thinking it would be wonderful if it ever happened.

'Considering it's not long since you and Martin broke up, I'm surprised at how contented you seem. Have you two made it up? Is that it?'

'No,' Claire hesitated, wondering whether she should let her sister know about Adam. It wouldn't hurt. After all, Liz knew no-one from her school, so it wouldn't matter, but then superstitiously she decided it was too soon even to tell her. 'Martin wasn't right for me,' she added. 'I should never have agreed to marry him.'

'I suppose that's why you look so cheerful, you're relieved it's all over?'

'Something like that,' Claire replied.

'Well, I hope you find someone else soon, you're not getting any younger. You'll be thirty soon.'

'Thanks for reminding me,' Claire laughed. 'Anyway, you look marvellous yourself. Being a mum suits you.'

'I still feel exhausted, but it's early days yet. I've been very lucky. Brian is so good with Melissa, he helps with everything and my friend, Sara, has been here a lot. She would have come round this weekend, but it's her birthday and she's gone away for a few days.'

'I'd like to meet her.'

'You'll do so at the christening. That will probably be Christmas. I'll make sure it's during the school holidays so you can come.'

'Thanks, Liz. I'll look forward to that.'

She kissed her sister. 'Claire, I hope that one day you'll be as happy as us.'

'Don't worry about me, I am happy.' That's the truth she thought. I feel as if I have been re-born.

Claire and Adam kept in touch by phone when she returned to Greenhill. It was arranged that the following Saturday which was her thirtieth birthday, she would visit him at his home in Springwood. They planned to have lunch there and then drive into the countryside for the rest of the day.

On the morning of her birthday Claire awoke to the sound of rain pattering down her bedroom window. By the time Adam came to collect her there was a storm raging and their plans had to be changed.

He presented her with a bouquet of red roses and a little box containing a gold herringbone necklace which he asked her to wear.

'It's beautiful,' she breathed. 'Thank you so much.' She flung her arms around him, holding on tightly as if she were afraid that he might disappear before her eyes.

'This is just the start,' Adam said at last. 'We've the whole day ahead of us to enjoy. I think the storm is passing.'

He was wrong however. The rain continued for the rest of the morning, but they didn't care, they were so pleased to be together. They went to Adam's house in Springwood. He showed Claire round the neat well decorated rooms and she gazed out at the attractive garden. 'I didn't know you liked gardening,' she remarked.

'There are a lot of things you don't know about me,' he answered.

While he was in the kitchen preparing their lunch, Claire looked around the lounge. She was surprised there were no photos of Beth anywhere.

After they'd eaten she mentioned this.

'I did have some pictures on display. I removed them from the bookcase yesterday. I wasn't sure what your reaction would be if I left them there.'

'I'd love to see them, Adam.'

He got up from the table and returned a few moments later, carrying a large envelope. 'You look at those while I clear up.'

'Can I help you?'

'No. It won't take long. I'll put the dishwasher on and make us a drink.'

'That was a lovely meal,' Claire remarked. 'You're a good cook.'

'I've had to be,' he said wryly.

'Of course,' she murmured, wishing she'd kept quiet. She didn't want to do or say anything that would spoil the day.

Adam went into the kitchen and Claire opened the envelope. She took the photos out one by one and stared at them in fascination.

So this was Adam's wife. She was very pretty, quite delicate looking, Claire thought. Suddenly she felt overcome with sadness for this young woman who was smiling so happily beside Adam on her wedding day, unaware of the terrible tragedy that would soon befall her.

The last photograph Claire picked up was of Beth sitting in her hospital bed cuddling a tiny, cherubic baby. Claire choked back a sob as Adam returned carrying a tray of drinks.

He quickly put it down and rushed over, folding her into his arms. 'I didn't mean to upset you. I'd forgotten that photo was there with the others.'

'Your baby was so beautiful,' Claire whispered tearfully, 'and Beth too.'

'They both were,' he agreed, quietly wiping a tear from his own eye.

'I'm glad you showed them to me. It was all so tragic.'

'I'm afraid life is like that sometimes, so when we find happiness we must hang onto it.'

'You're right, Adam. I know that now.'

As it continued raining they spent the

rest of the afternoon chatting and listening to music. There was so much to talk about. They both had five years to catch up on.

In the evening they decided to go to the cinema in Greenhill. Claire couldn't concentrate on the film, partly because she was distracted by Adam being so close to her, but also because she was mulling over the events of the last few days. She wondered what he was thinking and whether he was enjoying the film.

Afterwards he said, 'That was a good film.'

'Yes, it was,' she agreed. 'This has been a lovely birthday even though it is my thirtieth.'

'It's not over yet,' Adam replied.

When they arrived back at Claire's flat she invited him in for a coffee. She made the drinks while he sat in the kitchen talking to her. Then they took them into the lounge.

Suddenly Adam put his hand into his pocket and pulled out a familiar little

blue box, which she recognised immediately.

'I'd like you to have this back,' he
said.

Claire's heart was beating so fast she
was afraid it would burst. With
trembling fingers, she opened the box.
There inside was the engagement ring
she'd sent back to Adam all those years
ago. He took it out and placed it on her
finger. 'Will you marry me, Claire?'

'You've kept the ring,' she breathed.

'Of course. I couldn't bear to part
with it. I always hoped that one day I
would be able to give it back to you.
What's your answer, Claire? Please
don't keep me in suspense any longer.'

'Yes, Adam! Oh yes.' She put her
arms around him, kissing his lips
fervently.

'Can it be soon?' he asked when they
paused for breath.

'Very soon, I can't wait.'

'Before I start my new job?'

'In the summer holiday if that's what
you want.' She burst out laughing. 'I'd

better start planning it now, we haven't got long. What are they going to say at school when they find out?'

'I neither know nor care. I just want to make you my wife as soon as possible. That was my third decision, to ask you to marry me.'

'And you did it with perfect timing, on my birthday. You have made a wonderful day even better. I'll remember this birthday for the rest of my life.'

'I hope you will.' Adam kissed Claire again holding her close and she felt overwhelmed with love for him. 'There's one more thing, I'd like to ask.'

'What's that?' Claire looked up at him.

'To make another dream come true, I'd like to sell my house in Springwood and look for one in Greenhill? What do you say?'

'I'd love that. Maybe we'll discover your grandparents' bungalow is for sale.'

'Now that would be wonderful, but

as long as I'm with you I don't really mind where we live.'

'As long as it's in Greenhill,' Claire added.

'Of course.'

'And Adam, I just want to say thank you for giving me a second chance.'

'Don't forget it's a second chance for me too.'

'No I won't ever forget,' Claire murmured as she snuggled back into Adam's arms.

THE END

We do hope that you have enjoyed reading this large print book.

Did you know that all of our titles are available for purchase?

We publish a wide range of high quality large print books including:
Romances, Mysteries, Classics
General Fiction
Non Fiction and Westerns

Special interest titles available in large print are:
The Little Oxford Dictionary
Music Book, Song Book
Hymn Book, Service Book

Also available from us courtesy of Oxford University Press:
Young Readers' Dictionary
(large print edition)
Young Readers' Thesaurus
(large print edition)

For further information or a free brochure, please contact us at:
Ulverscroft Large Print Books Ltd.,
The Green, Bradgate Road, Anstey,
Leicester, LE7 7FU, England.
Tel: (00 44) 0116 236 4325
Fax: (00 44) 0116 234 0205